TURMOIL IN THE WEAVER'S NEST

PETER HENKAL

≈ *the watermark press*

Turmoil in the Weaver's Nest

© Peter HenKal

First published in 2022
by The Watermark Press, Plettenberg Bay
All rights reserved.

Editing and project management by Mike Kantey
Design and layout by Sonja Kantey

Printed by BKBookbinders, Durban

ISBN 978-1-7764288-7-8

Chapter One

Kent and Carla Fowler

Today the view over the white, sandy beaches, tranquil blue waters, and distant mountains is utterly breath-taking.

Throttling back his Honda road-bike at the top of the steep driveway, Kent Fowler removes his helmet, unzips his leather jacket, and takes a deep breath of fresh sea air. His wife Carla is about 50 metres behind him on her slightly smaller Honda, carefully negotiating the speed bumps in the strictly 30 km/h zone of the luxury estate's access road. The couple's new home is on top of the ridge with unrestricted views over the Indian Ocean, less than a kilometre away as the crow flies – or should that be a seagull?

"No more cityscapes and smog for me," Carla says, pulling off her helmet and shaking out the long tresses of her hair as blonde as wheat. Using his fingers to comb his own, short-cropped hair, infused with streaks of silver-grey, Kent watches as Carla shrugs off her leather jacket, carelessly slinging it over the bike's handlebars.

"Finally," she says, stretching her limbs, "the day has come."

"It took the builders long enough," he responds, his clear blue eyes hardening. "I thought we'd never get to move in here." He opens the triple-garage doors at the bottom of the driveway with his remote and rides carefully down the driveway in search of a spot for the heavy bike next to the mountain of packing-cases.

"Will you please get my bike down for me?" says Carla. "I don't trust myself on this steep driveway just yet."

"Sure, give me a moment to move some of these boxes," he replies.

The construction has taken far longer, and cost nearly 50 percent more than they had anticipated. The price you pay when you build a new house over one thousand kilometres away from your business, he tries to console himself, but the stress has left its mark: they are both exhausted. To top it all, Carla's parents had recently arrived on a long-planned holiday from Denmark before the house had been ready for them to move in. Kent gets on well with his in-laws, but the visit should have been delayed by at least three months. Too late now: just grin and bear it, he thinks.

Barely fifteen minutes later; with the first packing case half unpacked, his phone crows. With a quick glance at the screen, he answers: "Yes Bobby, talk to me."

He listens, eyes widening in disbelief.

"When? ... Is he alright? ... Thank God for that! How much did they take off him? ... Shit! Okay, I'll catch the next plane. I'll text you my arrival time once I have a ticket."

Kent pockets the phone and turns to Carla.

"Dumisani got held up on his way to the bank with last night's takings," he says. "He is alright: just some heavy bruises where they hit him with a piece of pipe before kicking him. I am going back up to L'Afrique; they need me up there. Maybe I can get a late-afternoon or early-evening flight."

"Oh, Kent," she says, her frustration sharpening her voice. "That's not the first time. Didn't you tell them repeatedly that two men are needed to go to the bank? When do you think you'll come back?"

He turns, hesitates, takes a deep breath, and says: "Carla, I am not coming back!"

Chapter Two

Carla

As Kent rides off on her smaller Honda without looking back, Carla slumps onto one of the packing cases. He will have gone to pack some of his belongings at their temporary apartment the four of them had been forced to rent while waiting for the final touches to their house.

He is joking, is Carla's first reaction. They have known each other for 40 years and have been married for 32. What the hell is he talking about?'

But then she admits: Things have not been sailing smoothly over the last year, or maybe even longer. She had put it down to stress, brought on by her decision to sell her lucrative hairdressing salon, the sale of their old house in the eastern suburbs: all designed to raise the capital to build this place. Then there were the day-to-day demands of the family's liquor stores; Kent's Nightclub – the man has never stopped. They hardly spent time together anymore. Carla's only consolation have been the dogs – only one left now; her beautiful German Shepherd Lex – a true companion: rock solid, and so protective.

Two years before, they had decided to buy a property on the North Coast of Natal so that they might delegate some responsibilities to his senior managers and take things a bit more easily. It had sounded so good: walks on the beach, a chance to relax, recapture and revitalise their relationship.

At first, they had taken an option and paid a hefty deposit on an apartment in a complex under development in Ballito Bay. Only 700 kilometres from his business, it had seemed a relatively easy commute by car or plane but that development had never got off the ground and their lawyer was still trying to retrieve the deposit from the now insolvent developer.

Later, on a bike trip to the Cape, they had come across this luxury complex with a few prime plots still up for sale. Overlooking the most amazing coastline and surrounded by blue mountains, one of its last available plots had been irresistible. After weighing up all the pros – and not enough of the cons – they bought that expensive view site to build their dream home. That had added brand-new, untold stress, while travelling back and forth over 1,400 kilometres was no longer an easy commute.

False promises and poor project management by the architect had brought the build to a halt several times. Costly mistakes in the early stages of excavation on the steep site had further caused huge cost overruns and time delays – all because Kent had not been there at these crucial stages.

The budget, the bloody budget! Cut back here and cut back there. As the project bookkeeper, it had become her job to scrape every penny together and she was heartily sick of it. For what purpose had she slaved away for all those bloody years in her salon? Now her money had become part of this project! Eaten up by delay after delay.

What will she tell her parents, who are back at the rented apartment, loading more boxes into her Mercedes Estate to bring across here? Both in their 80s, Christian and Anna Carstens had come all the way from Denmark to celebrate the move into the new home with Kent and her.

First the house had not been ready and now, to crown it all: "Sorry, folks, but your son-in-law has just left me." No way, I can't say a word now. Have to keep it to myself.

Just then, the white Mercedes Estate, driven by her father, turns off the service road, down the steep driveway to the entrance of the triple garage.

"What happened?" asks her father Christian, sliding slowly from behind the steering wheel. "Kent was in such a hurry – packing his things, phoning for a taxi – all we could get out of him was something about a robbery and problems with the business he needs to attend to urgently."

"How long is he going to be gone?" Carla's mother Anna chimes in. "Will we still see him before we go back to Denmark?"

Kent obviously hasn't said anything about not coming back.

"I don't know, Ma," says Carla, "he can only tell me once he is on top of things again. He also wants to sell one of our business properties to raise more funds to finish this place off."

"He will, I am sure," says Christian, who holds his son-in-law in very high esteem.

Carla quickly turns away to open the rear passenger door, where the muzzled Lex is straining to get out.

"Lex, sit! Stay!" Carla commands in a loud voice; taking hold of his lead as he jumps off the rear passenger seat.

She takes the highly excited Lex to her new bedroom and locks him into his steel holding pen, not wanting to let him loose on their yet unfenced property. The last thing she needs in her life is trouble with her new neighbours.

Damn you, Kent! she thinks. *How can you do this to me? If this is your idea of a joke, it's sick, really sick.*

But something deep down inside tells her: This is not a joke.

Chapter Three

Kent

The taxi driver glances at his fare in the interior rear-view mirror. His passenger is shaking so badly, the driver can feel the vibration through the back of his seat.

"Are you alright, *meneer*?' he asks with genuine concern in his voice.

"I'm okay," says Kent, trying to bring the raging adrenalin under control. "One of my managers got mugged on the way to the bank with last night's takings," he says.

"Shit," says the driver, focusing on the traffic, as the freeway passes through a settlement with a 60-km speed restriction.

Changing the subject to the real issue on his mind, Kent says: "Are you married?"

"Ja, *meneer*, ten years this year, two children, boy and a girl," says the driver, speeding up as they exit the village, "and you, sir?"

"I just threw the towel in after thirty-two years," says Kent, starting to shake again.

"You're joking? Thirty-two years, and you split, because why?" says the driver.

"Too long a story to tell you between here and the airport," says Kent warily, sinking back into the seat, and trying hard to control the shaking. They say nothing more until they stop at the tiny airport.

"Really sorry to hear about your separation, *meneer*," says the driver finally, handing Kent his luggage.

"Yeah, sure ... thanks," mumbles Kent, adding a generous tip to his fare.

"Thank you, sir, *en jammer, né*? Take care."

"The next flight to Oliver Tambo International is in three hours' time." Kent is told by the booking clerk. He takes his ticket and makes his way through the small airport to the seating area, which is blissfully empty being so far ahead of the next scheduled departure. He buys a can of Liquifruit from the dispenser and settles into one of the seats near the window overlooking the runway.

Why today? he asks himself. Maybe the mugging triggered it off — the last straw — or maybe it provided a good enough excuse to finally get away.

Why did I wait so long? Having thought about it a lot, he had just wanted to make sure that Carla would be alright and where she had always longed to be: at the coast, in a nice home. Why not? He owed her that much and she would be 1,200 kilometres away from him not in his back yard.

He gets up, helps himself to another can of fruit juice, and sits back down, still the only one in the seating area.

What will I tell my parents?

Graham and Dorothy Fowler had emigrated to South Africa from the UK in the early 1950s. A brewer's son, Graham had followed in his father's footsteps and worked for one of the big UK Breweries, servicing the liquor outlets and local pubs in the Midlands. Arriving in South Africa, he had started as a salesman for South African Breweries. Then young and ambitious, he had opened his own bottle store on the East Rand, outside of Johannesburg.

Having done well, he had then made sure that his only son, Kent, had received a good education. Kent in return had been expected to help in the bottle store on Friday afternoons and Saturday mornings and at age 18, with his schooling completed, he had joined his father full-time in the store. The younger man's job had been to control the stock rooms and restock the fridges. Although it had been hard work, Kent had enjoyed hefting the crates and boxes, which was not unlike working out in a gym. Catching two birds with one stone, he had thought.

Measuring nearly two metres tall and weighing in at 95 kg of solid muscle, the girls gave him appraising looks, but his greater passion lay in music. More precisely, he wanted to become a disc jockey in his spare time.

In 1977, the appearance of the movie *Saturday Night Fever* had changed the music scene in South Africa: live music was forever eclipsed by professional, celebrity DJs becoming the epicentre of highly orchestrated and brightly lit discotheques. Kent had spent all his free evenings in dance clubs – neither dancing nor drinking; nor taking drugs nor picking up girls but standing close to the DJs and watching them work their turntables: especially the way they selected certain cuts by judging the mood of the crowd on the dance floor, keeping them dancing with beat after beat after disco beat.

During the day, Kent continued working well with his father and soon they had discussed opening a second liquor outlet, followed by a third, and a fourth. Kent invested in his own disco equipment and converted the garage into an imaginary nightclub stage. By covering the walls and garage door with egg trays, and keeping the volume low, so as not to upset the neighbours, he could practise every night after dinner, until midnight.

When he thought he was ready, he went to local clubs for auditions: first in the East Rand, close to home, then in central Johannesburg. Finally, he received his break in the booming, upmarket club scene of the more affluent Northern Suburbs. His DJ name came naturally. His surname of "Fowler" became "Fowl" at first, and then the more masculine "Rooster", accompanied by his trademark opening of the sunrise crowing cockerel. As "DJ Rooster" he became famous and started pulling in big crowds – and big money. With his direct connection to the family's liquor stores, he offered the clubs bigger discounts than they received elsewhere. Business was booming. Kent was a very, very busy man, with not much time to himself, but he did not mind. He had his music and made more money than he had ever expected to make at this young age, while the emerging "Rainbow Nation" under the legendary Nelson Mandela had offered yet more opportunities to him.

On one of those rare Sunday afternoons when they were not at work and had come together as a family for a traditional South African *braai*, or barbecue, Old Man Fowler pulled Kent aside. Pointing up into a tree he said: "It's time to stop thinking like a rooster. Look at that bright-yellow bird, all speckled in brown that is busy building an upside-down home. Look at how he hangs upside down as he pulls and tugs different strands of grass and thin twigs to form a perfect shelter: the weaver's nest.

"That must be your goal: to build nests. Use your own and all our resources to buy the properties that we currently rent for our liquor stores. Move into new territories in the south-western townships. Buy the properties, open liquor stores, open your own nightclub. You have a huge following. Lure them in – just like the weaver bird lures his female into the completed nest."

Kent had sat there, watching the brightly coloured bird flitting back and forth, weaving its nest. Finally, he had risen to his feet, bade his family "good night" and had gone to work.

A gentle touch on his shoulder by one of the airport workers rouses him. "Mr Fowler? Your flight is boarding now."

Kent looks around, totally disorientated for a moment. "Thanks," he says, rubbing his eyes, before grabbing his slim briefcase to board the plane. Settling into a comfortable seat, he is grateful that the seat next to his remains empty.

The last thing he needs is for some person wanting to engage in the usual small talk that takes place on flights. Having declined the stewardess's offer of a drink or snack, he tilts his seat back and shuts his eyes.

During the last few years, he and his father had gradually bought the properties in which their liquor stores were accommodated and had rented out the spaces they did not require themselves.

One day, their newly formed property-management company CEO, Thomas Banks, asked Kent to look at a newly listed building in the central business district of Johannesburg's Southern Suburbs. Ideally suited for a liquor store, the then current owner had already obtained the necessary licence but – having suffered a sudden stroke – had been forced to sell. The location was excellent, the three-floor building was in good repair and boasted an ample parking lot.

"What do you think?" Thomas had asked.

"Let's go inside," insisted Kent.

Large empty floors, lifts, stairways, fire escapes ... "It's got potential," Kent admitted, his mind visualising the layout.

Ground floor: Liquor store; First Floor: bar/cocktail lounge with a kitchen for light meals, billiard tables etc. Top floor: the disco; his own disco: "DJ Rooster's Club L'Afrique." How long had he dreamed about his own club!

"Check out the by-laws," he tells Thomas. "Being part of a

business district, will noise be a problem? Check with sound-proofing companies what they can bring the decibel level down to. See what you can negotiate."

Kent continued to move around on the third floor as if in a trance. Yes, my own "DJ Rooster's Club L'Afrique." Little did he know at that time how that day would shape the rest of his life.

The rumbling and vibration of the landing-gear being lowered shakes Kent out of his semi-slumbering state. Drowsily, he glances down at the lights of the city below. As the plane descends, he can make out familiar landmarks, until they land on the runway with a series of soft bumps, and the engines are roaring in reverse thrust.

Kent collects his luggage from the carousel in the Arrival's Hall and makes his way to the Exit. Just a few metres away, he sees his silver-grey Porsche Cayenne Turbo is parked with its distinctive "DJ Rooster's Club L'Afrique" logo. He can also make out the anxious face of his assistant club manager, Dumisani Dlamini, peering through the side window.

Seeing Kent approaching, Dumisani jumps out with a plaster on the side of his face and bruises around his eyes. "Hi, Boss," he says solemnly in greeting. "Give me your bags." No big smile tonight.

Kent gets behind the wheel and adjusts his seat to accommodate his long legs. With Dumisani next to him in the front passenger seat, he guns the engine and swerves into the stream of traffic leaving the airport concourse.

"Talk to me, Dumi," he demands, cutting lanes to get to the N1 highway on-ramp.

"Well," says Dumisani, looking forlornly at Kent, "we were busy, the cocktail floor was still buzzing with an unusually big lunchtime crowd – some company birthday party. It was coming up to closing time for the banks and Bobby was keeping an eye on the noisy party, so I took the satchel, and went to the bank. I have done it many times before ..."

"Yes, and I told you as many times before NOT to go alone. We got no bloody insurance cover, only if two employees go, remember?" interrupts Kent. "So then, what happened?" "Two scooters jammed me, the two back-seat guys jumped me, hit me with a piece of pipe, and kicked me down, ripped the satchel off me, and jumped back onto the scooters as the drivers roared off. People just stood and stared when I got up and screamed."

"You were lucky they didn't stab or shoot you," says Kent. "How much was in the satchel?"

"Twenty-eight thousand," Dumisani mutters. "Shit," says Kent, trying to keep his temper.

"I'll pay it back," Dumisani assures him. "I'll work extra hours … I'm sorry, Boss."

Kent gives him a quick, hard look. He likes his team: they are solid, reliable guys who have been with him through a lot.

What do they say? "Shit happens!"

Robert "Bobby" Ncobo – just under two metres tall and weighing in at 125 kg – gives Kent a bear hug when he enters the manager's office on the top floor, pulling the door closed behind him to drown out the noise of the club floor.

"Hey, Kent, sorry about this," the manager says. "No excuses. It's my fault. I shouldn't have let him go by himself. Never again, I swear. I will pay back every penny to you, I promise."

"Enough promises," says Kent. "Dumi offered to pay; you offered to pay – at that rate I'll be very happy, if you guys were knocked over the head every week. Then I'll get paid back twice!"

You can feel the tension leave the room as the three of them look at each other, slow smiles creeping back onto their faces.

"How long are you here for?" Bobby asks.

"For good," Kent snaps back. "It looks like I need to babysit you guys, don't I?"

Changing the subject abruptly, he says: "Who is spinning the discs tonight?"

"DJ Hot Stuff – I mean Tanya – is on tonight," Dumi says with a little crooked smile peeping through a swollen lower lip. "The place is packed out: she's got them eating out of her hand."

"Okay, see you later," says Kent and goes to his own office/ bedroom to change. The sparse bedroom saves him the ride home in the early morning hours.

A nightclub is a nightclub: it often plays Cupid to romantic, sometimes illicit, relationships. The staff all know the drill. Keep your mouth shut, look the other way, mind your own business, and get on with the job!

Five minutes later, Kent joins Tanya at the mixing tables, gives her a quick hug, picks up the headphones, sets up the second mixer with his Rooster signature tune, and fades Tanya's table out.

"It's the Rooster!" he crows.

For the next hour, the two DJs spin Club L'Afrique into a frenzy. Kent can feel the tension draining from him. Tomorrow has just begun! Drenched in perspiration, they towel their faces as the lights dim and the crowd begins reluctantly to leave the club.

Tanya grins at Kent and says: "Hi, Rooster. Nice to have you share the stage with me again. How long this time?"

"This time ..." he hesitates before saying, "for good!"

Tanya throws him a quizzical look as he skips off the stage and makes for the exit.

Chapter Four

Carla

Carla and her parents finally manage to clear the last of the boxes out of the temporary accommodation, clean the place up, and return the key to the agency. Bit by bit, they manage to get the new house into a state resembling something close to orderly, when disaster strikes. The global pandemic of the Corona virus (known as "Covid-19") arrives, the South African President Cyril Ramaphosa declares a State of Emergency, and a complete lockdown of the country, as do many countries throughout the world.

"How are we going to get home?" wails Anna, Carla's mother.

Carla tries to reassure her. "Don't worry; it will pass. You are better off here, anyway."

More reports come in from their older daughter, Theresa who lives in Copenhagen. "Things are not good here," she writes. "I advise you to stay with Carla until we can be sure your health is not threatened here."

Christian and Anna Carstens had emigrated to South Africa in 1957, lured by the prospects offered by a rapidly developing country. As a qualified tool- and die-maker, Christian had found a position immediately, which included a company house, as was customary in those days, a tradition carried over from the goldmines that operated all around Johannesburg.

Theresa was born in 1958, followed by Carla in 1960. Raised in a strict, but loving home, the two girls had then progressed through well-protected school years. Theresa, quiet and studious, had gone on to university to obtain her Bachelor of Commerce degree to become an accountant.

Carla, a more free-spirited rebel, wanted to become a hairdresser. Aged 16, she had been hired as an apprentice hairdresser by a woman called Sonja, who had operated a busy salon in a small, popular shopping centre, next door to Fowler Liquor store. It was there that Carla had first seen Kent, opening the store in the mornings, loading and off-loading trucks during the day, and closing the store at night. His very short-cropped, dark hair made it difficult to determine his age, but his muscular build, broad shoulders, narrow hips, and tight jeans suggested he was in his twenties. When Sonja caught Carla craning her neck to get a better look one morning, she laughed out loud and said: "That's Kent Fowler, the son, better known as 'DJ Rooster'. He is hot!

I have seen him perform at Raffles in the city and he sure can pull in a crowd. You should go see him."

"I can't," says Carla, "I'm not eighteen and my parents won't let me."

Then, not long after that conversation, an unexpected opportunity arose when Christian called the sisters together. "Theresa, Carla, we are going away to a convention for the weekend. You girls are old enough to look after yourselves. Lock up when it gets dark. With our dogs in the yard, you have nothing to be afraid of."

"Of course, Papa," said Theresa, "no problem: we will be fine."

"Sonja, guess what?" said Carla on the following morning in the salon. "My parents are going away for the weekend. Will you take me with you to Raffles on Saturday night? I want to see him." She pointed over her shoulder at Kent, who was just coming out of the bottle store.

"Sure," said Sonja. "We are three or four: one more won't make any difference. Do you have high heels? We will tease up your hair to make you look taller and with a bit more make-up you'll be fine. I know the guy at the door, anyway: he wants to get into my pants, If I distract him, he won't even look at you." Then Sonja laughed and pushed her ample breasts up a little higher. "See what I mean?"

The problem, however, would remain with Theresa: would she be agreeable?

That night, after dinner, Carla had approached Theresa in her bedroom.

"Can I come in and talk to you for a moment?" Carla asked when Theresa looked up from her books.

"Yes, come in," said Theresa, far friendlier than at other times when Carla had interrupted her. "What's on your mind?"

"I want to go out with Sonja and some of her friends on Saturday night," the younger sister stammered.

"Do you really?" Theresa replied with a little smile. "Well, that suits me."

"What? You mean I can go?" Carla gasped, not believing what she was hearing. But hmm ... What do you mean that it 'suits you'?"

"Well," said Theresa, looking at the door to make sure they couldn't be heard. "I want to bring a boy over."

"You what?!" Carla spluttered, "to sleep over?"

"Shush! Not so loud. Yes, to sleep over. Do you mind? I am nearly 19, you know," she added.

"Papa will kill you," Carla grimaced.

"Are you going to tell him?" Theresa retorted with a wicked little smile.

"Of course not," Carla said and winked at her older sister, before returning to her own room. *Yes! I am going to see the Rooster!* She smiled and hugged herself.

After the last client had left the salon, Sonja washed Carla's flaxen hair and wove it into a nest of strands and tumbling curls, cascading down to her shoulders.

"Now, be careful," Sonja admonished the younger woman. "Don't pull anything over your head; wear a button- up top and leave some buttons open."

"You are wicked!" Carla laughed. Ten minutes later, make-up done, she certainly looked much older.

At 7.30 p.m. sharp, Sonja arrived in her Toyota with two other girls, Pat and Angela, who came to the salon regularly.

"Hi," said Carla, "I am so excited! Aren't you?"

"Well, yes, but we go every week, you know. We are sort of regulars."

"You go every week?" Carla said in awe.

"Yes, only when the Rooster is on," Pat replied. "I've got a crush on him, but he is so into his music, he doesn't even look at me. Maybe he is queer. You can't tell, with his cropped hair and skin-tight jeans. I get wet just looking at him."

"Oh, really?" Carla murmured. *So I am not the only one.*

The doorman had drawn Sonja closer to him and whispered something into her ear. Pushing the others through the door, she had giggled and put her arms around him. "Later ... Easy does it!"

Carla was in! They had looked around for a table near the dance floor. Since it had been early still, they had been in luck and had taken their seats, before ordering drinks from the waitress that had greeted them with a welcoming smile.

"Back, again?" she said, while turning to Carla, she added: "Hi, I'm Maxine, we haven't met before."

"Hi, Maxine. I'm Carla. I work for Sonja," she replied.

"I like your hair," the waitress remarked. "It looks like a weaver's nest."

They all laughed until a moment later when the taped music faded and a spotlight hit the turntables above the dance floor, followed by the loud crowing of a rooster.

"And now, ladies and gentlemen, here is the one and only DJ Rooster!"

After another burst of loud crowing, a pencil spot illuminated the short-cropped head of Kent Fowler.

Then the music started, together with the dipping and swirling of coloured spots, punctuated by pulsating strobe lights. Conversation was then impossible, so Pat and Angie stood up to dance. Sonja pulled Carla onto the floor, pushing her forward toward the small stage. DJ Rooster gave Sonja a wave of recognition, then smiled and winked at Carla.

With her doting glance fixed on the DJ, Carla had not noticed the wildly gyrating youngster that had pushed his way between her and Sonja. Only when she felt his hand on her arm, attempting to swirl her around in time with the thumping rhythm, did she realise that Sonja had joined Pat and Angie, leaving her to the imposing dancer.

Bewildered, she scuttled over to the dancing trio. "Don't you dare leave me!" she tried to communicate to Sonja, but the loud music drowned out her words. Angie, Pat, and Sonja, all familiar with the latest dance routines, pulled Carla into a straight line. Entwining their arms, they proceeded, two steps to the left, one forward, two steps to the right, and one back, all singing in time to the chorus. Hardly stopping for a quick sip of their drinks, the four women danced in a close group, pushing would-be intruders out of the way. On their way home, hours later, Carla was a little disappointed. Sure, she had enjoyed the dancing, but had hoped to get more than a quick smile and a wink from the Rooster.

A couple of days later, Carla had seen Kent locking up again. she had dropped the broom promptly and run out of the salon.

"Hi, Rooster, I saw you the other night at Raffles. Well, I think you are really good," she said, blushing a deep red.

"And I think you are ..." he grinned, "cute, yes, cute. How long are you going to be? Fancy an ice-cream float?"

"Sure, thanks, I mean, yes, please ... er ... give me ten minutes," she said, not trusting her own voice.

Running back into the salon she pleaded with her boss. "Sonja, quick, quick! Let me finish. HE asked me out, quick!" By this time Carla was close to screaming.

"Give me that broom," Sonja laughed. "I'll finish the job but go and do your hair first: you look like a kitchen mop."

With shaking hands, Carla pummelled her long, blonde tresses into some sort of order. "Thanks!" she shouted in her excitement. "See you tomorrow!" And she was gone.

Kent was waiting for her in one of Fowlers Liquor Emporium's delivery vans.

"Is this what you drive?" she asked, getting in next to him.

"Yes, do you like it?" Then he grinned, after appraising her appearance. "Do you always look like this?"

"Excuse me," she said indignantly, "I have just got off work."

"Me, too," he said grinning all over again as they drove out of the parking lot.

Their first date, then, sipping iced milkshakes at a drive-in, fast-food eatery had been anything but romantic. He had asked most of the usual questions: about her family, her hobbies, and her plans in the future.

"I want to become the best hairdresser in town with my own salon," she had replied with such conviction that he could only believe her. "Sonja is very good and has won a couple of championships. She wants to send me on training courses with Kérastase, our hair-product supplier. She also wants to send me on an internship at Carlton Hair in the Northern Suburbs where the rich and famous have their hair done.

"Sonja was with Carlton before she went solo," Carla had continued, barely stopping to catch a breath. "What about you?" she asked Kent.

"Me and my old man are expanding Fowlers Liquor Emporium and investing in properties that house our stores," he replied.

"And your DJ Rooster business?" she asked. "You are so popular, you could just do that full-time, couldn't you?"

"I could, but my dad and I have bigger plans that include my own nightclub," he responded, looking straight into her sparkling, brown eyes which were most unusual for a blonde. The intense look he gave her with his clear, blue eyes gave her butterflies in the stomach.

"You mean like Raffles?" she asked in awe.

"No, much bigger and better," he replied so convincingly that she believed him, but a quick glance at her watch brought her back to reality.

"I must go," she sighed. "It's dinner time and our family dinners are like holy communion. Sorry, but can you take me home?"

"Sure, can we go to a movie tomorrow night?" he asked. "You have to ask my parents," she replied, feeling herself blush with embarrassment, "and they will most probably insist that my older sister Theresa comes with us."

"Why? How old are you?" he asked.

"Nearly seventeen," she said, blushing even more.

"But you were in Raffles the other night," he protested, somewhat surprised.

"Sonja smuggled me in," Carla said in return. "She distracted the door guy with her boobs."

Kent burst out laughing and then said, "I will come for you at 7.30 in the evening and ask your folks. Is that all right?"

"Yes, I hope so," she said. "You are the first boy to do that," and then blushed for the third time.

After he had dropped her off at home, she had been questioned closely by her mother, who had watched them through the kitchen window.

"Was that the Fowler boy who gave you a lift home?" she had asked.

"Yes, Mother. We met in the parking lot and he offered me a lift," Carla replied.

"But in that case, you should have been home earlier than

now," her mother said, looking at her wristwatch.

"He bought me an iced milkshake at the drive-in."

"I see," had been her mother's stern reply.

On the following evening at exactly 7.30 p.m., they had heard a polite knock on the door.

"It's for me!" Carla had shouted, rushing to open the door.

Kent was standing there, a bunch of flowers in his hand, dressed in a clean pair of jeans, a Polo shirt, and a suede-leather jacket.

"Hi. Does this pass?" he had whispered, squeezing her arm with one hand, flowers in the other.

She had giggled nervously. "Fool," she had teased him, "What's with the flowers? Are you going to ask for my hand?"

"May as well," he grinned. "It will save me buying another bunch in a couple of years' time."

"What do you mean?" she said.

"Just what I said," he says, grinning his wicked grin once again.

Sitting in the front parlour, Mr and Mrs Carstens got up when they recognised Kent and saw the flowers in his hand.

"Good evening. These are for you, Mrs Carstens," he said, handing the flowers to her. "I am Kent Fowler. We have met before at the bottle store, I am sure." Turning to her husband, he continued by addressing him directly. "May I take Carla to the movies? Of course, Theresa can accompany us, she is most welcome to sit in the jump seat."

"What do you mean by the jump seat, Kent?" Mr Carstens asked.

"I drive a Porsche 911," he said in all seriousness. "It is a two-seater with a small jump seat in the rear."

"I see," said Mr Carstens. "Well, in that case, that won't be necessary. I can't really expect her to sit there all scrunched up, breathing down your necks," and then he smiled for the first time.

"Thank you, Papa," Carla bubbled forth in her excitement. "Bye, see you later."

"Pumpkin time is at midnight; work tomorrow," said her mother, while looking around for a place to put the vase after she had arranged the flowers.

The rest was history. They had courted for three years; had married, all the while pursuing their ambitious plans. Carla had enrolled in courses and sought internships at Carlton Hair, going on to winning the world hairdressing championship in California. She had then returned home to buy Sonja out, when the latter fell pregnant and decided to pack it in, being always on the go, and barely stopping for a breath of air.

Graham and Kent had continued in expanding the family business. They had bought the properties which had housed the various Fowler Liquor Emporia and had also bought the building that now housed Kent's own Club L'Afrique.

Everything had been coming up roses, until ... when exactly?

<h1 style="text-align:center">Chapter Five</h1>

<h2 style="text-align:center">Kent</h2>

"Kent, it's Dad, have you closed up?" says Graham, uncharacteristically without a greeting.

"Yes, Dad. Good morning. I closed up straight after the President's announcement. The club and all the stores are closed."

"Good. Let's meet with all the managers in Thomas Bank's office in Rosebank: it's the most central for all. Shall we say 2 p.m.?"

"Sure, Dad. See you, bye," says Kent and sends a WhatsApp to a group of all the bottle-store managers. Immediately afterwards, he decides to send a message to Tanya.

"Got time for coffee?"

"Always. Where?"

"Your place in 15 minutes?"

"I'll put the kettle on."

Fifteen minutes later Kent parks his silver-grey Porsche Cayenne Turbo in the courtyard of Tanya's apartment building. Taking three steps at a time he climbs the four flights of stairs and gives her door a sharp rap.

"It's open. Come on in," he hears her melodic voice. "Hey, this is Jo'burg: anybody ever tell you to keep your doors locked?" Kent admonishes.

"And top of the mornings to you, too," she says entwining her long bare legs with his and kissing him languidly before pushing him into his favourite recliner, and handing him his mug of steaming, black coffee. "What's up?" she asks as he takes his first sip.

"Graham and I are having a contingency meeting with all the store and club managers to discuss strategy. It's going to be tough for a while, I guess. We will have to see what develops.

"I am not so concerned about the business, because we are big enough to ride it for a while. My concern is the staff. The government promises relief, but you know how slow the wheels are turning: we need to find ways to help some of them."

"I can help," says Tanya without hesitation.

"You?" says Kent, "the club is closed, you are out of a job, how can you help?"

"Rooster, Rooster, Rooster – you are just a little farmyard cockerel, but I am the globe-trotting DJ Hot Stuff ..."

Kent interrupts. "There'll be no more globe-trotting with the globe locked down, Tanya."

She throws her shock of auburn hair back and boasts. "Unlike you, DJ Rooster, I am an international remixer to the famous, and in great demand. While you lift cases of booze up and down during the day, I remix for record studios and recording artists. At least allow me to help my colleagues in the club."

Kent looks at her appreciatively before taking the last sip of his coffee. Dropping the mug off in the open-plan kitchen on his way out, he hears her calling after him. "See you later, alligator."

What an unselfish person! he thinks as he descends, three steps at a time.

"Who would have thought we'd all walk around as if we are about to rob a bank," Kent says, entering the meeting room in their property management offices; bumping elbows with his father, and Thomas; giving high air-shakes to the other, barely recognisable group in front of him. Settling himself down next to Bobby, he looks expectantly at his father, who, as Chairman of the Board, is seated at the head of the table.

"Good afternoon," Graham begins. "We are waiting to receive details from the Liquor Board and can't do anything until further notice. Fortunately, our financial situation is strong: our books are well within the 60 to 90 days granted to us by our suppliers. They are going to start pushing us eventually, but for once we have a legitimate excuse. I would be happy to hear your concerns."

Thomas raises his hand fractionally off the table. When Graham nods in his direction, he says: "I foresee difficulties in collecting the rent from shop lessees that have no income."

"Let's cross that bridge when we come to it. We are not smarting yet, so let's agree to sit it out," says Graham. "Yes Bobby?" he turns to the night club manager.

"Boss, doesn't this remind you of the Prohibition in the United States?"

"I don't know, Bobby, a bit before my time. What are you getting at?"

"Well," says the giant, "from what I read, more booze was sold during, than before and after it was illegal." As some of the liquor store managers nod their heads in agreement, he continues. "Liquor stores were illegal for ages in the townships, yet everybody could buy booze 24/7 in shebeens and drink it right there or wrap the bottle in a brown-paper bag and sneak home with it." The older generation nod their heads in agreement.

"So?" asks Graham, "what are you getting at?"

Bobby laughs, stretching right back in his chair, he says: "Gentlemen, you know nothing, just leave your warehouse keys on the table on your way out: I'll *SHRINK* your stock for you."

There is a hush in the room, until Graham says: "Thanks for the suggestion, Bobby, but we will not gamble with our liquor licence. Once lost, it is near impossible to retrieve. We will do it 100 percent by the book. Thank you all for coming, guys. We'll keep you informed every day."

When only Graham, Thomas, Kent and his two club managers are left around the table, Kent looks at Bobby and says: "How were you going to pull that stunt off, Bobby?"

"Pull what off, Rooster?" the giant asks, pulling his Balaclava down so that only his white eyeballs are showing. Pointing his straightened index finger at Kent he sings: *"Bang, bang, I shot you down, bang, bang my baby shot me down ..."* and leaves the room.

As Dumisani rises to follow Bobby, Kent stops him: "Stay for a moment, I have a message from Hot Stuff for you," and he relates her offer to look after the club staff.

"Wow," says Dumi, choked for words, "where did you find that girl?"

"I didn't," says Kent, "she found us."

He elbow-bumps Dumi and says: "Keep in close contact with the club's staff: the waitresses will be hardest hit by the loss of their tips."

Turning to Thomas, he says: "Can you help me to get my house in the Cape transferred into Carla's name, I want her to own it outright."

His father looks at him, tears welling up in his eyes. Kent grabs him and hugs him hard to his chest. "Why, Kent, why, after 32 years?"

"I don't know, Dad, I really don't know."

Chapter Six

Leonora Sereno

Leonora started having her hair done by Carla when she read about the hairdresser winning the Hairdressing World Champion in California, in one of the glossy magazines: it may have been *Cosmopolitan,* or one like it, had phoned and made an appointment with Carla personally. During their first appointment, the two women had found out that they had gone to the same school, although Leonora had attended a couple of years later.

When the latter had finished high school, she had gone to study at Wits University and had earned her BA. Like many students she had shared a room with another student, called Angie, and had worked most nights as a waitress in an up-market restaurant nearby to subsidise the meagre allowance her parents could afford.

The Sereno family were refugees from Mozambique that had escaped with a couple of suitcases of clothing and not much else. Leonora's father had re-established himself in the wholesale fruit and vegetable market.

Leonora, an attractive, slender girl, with below shoulder-length, brown hair, had experienced several unsatisfactory liaisons with male students that had never gone very far.

"What am I doing wrong?" she had asked her roommate one night after yet another disappointing date with a third-year, law student. "Why do these guys think I am fair meat after one dinner in a cheap restaurant?"

Angela had shrugged sympathetically before saying: "They are all the same. I don't need guys anymore."

"What do you mean?" asks Leonora, moving over on their narrow settee to make space for Angela who had risen from her computer to sit beside her. Taking Leonora's hands into her own she had said: "One night I was invited to dinner at a friend's house. There were eight of us around the table: three couples, a young woman called Debra, and me. The conversation went through the usual boring topics, and I drank a little more than usual. Only when Debra and I went for a smoke break on the veranda, and the crisp winter air hit me, did I feel the full effect. I don't know if I stumbled, or lost my balance, but Debra pulled me close to steady me. Instead of apologising and letting go, I clung to her. A moment later we were kissing passionately and soon left to spend the night at Debra's."

When Leonora looked at Angela with an incredulous look in her eyes, Angela leant forward and kissed Leonora, whispering softly: "Just like this ..." When Leonora had woken in Angela's arms in the morning, moreover, her suspicion that she had not been attracted to men as lovers had been confirmed.

Through her early waitressing career Leonora had shifted to banqueting and event planning; eventually becoming an executive in an event management company. Her male partners, mostly gay, had put her in charge of sales. With her stunning looks, dry sense of humour, and reputation of delivering what she promised, she had no problems in securing large corporate clients.

What had sealed Leonora's and Carla's friendship forever took place during one of Leonora's weekly visits to Carla's salon.

During the usual exchange of trivial gossip, Leonora had said: "This new client insists that we get DJ Rooster for their event. I have tried everything, but his agent says he is fully booked six months ahead. It looks like I am not going to get this event, because they think I am no good."

"When is the event?" Carla asked, while blow-drying Leonora's shoulder-length hair.

"It's on a Tuesday, in two weeks' time," said Leonora, totally distraught.

"I'll speak to him tonight, I know he is free on Tuesdays," Carla said, twirling the brush under the flow of hot air.

"How can you possibly speak to the Rooster tonight? Don't tell me you know him," said Leonora.

"I sleep with him!"

"You what?"

"You heard right. I sleep with him every night: he is my husband," Carla smiled at Leonora, who was gulping for air.

"You are shitting me," she finally managed.

"Now, now, why would I do that? You are done. Go tell your client they will get DJ Rooster, but it will cost them plenty. Phone the agent and tell him I said to charge the client double for booking at short notice."

The two women had then embraced, and Leonora had dashed happily out of the salon.

Since that day, their friendship had gone from strength to strength. Even Kent had accepted Leonora into their circle of closest friends. The response to Covid-19, however – total lockdown, as well as social distancing – had left Leonora and her partners stranded. Like most industries, the event managers found themselves out of business overnight and she had needed time to re-organise and rethink her future.

"Hello Leonora," she hears Kent's familiar voice. "Can you speak?"

"Sure. Hi, Kent, talk to me," she says. Given all the drama associated with total lockdown, she had not had time to communicate with anybody other than her partners.

"Leonora," says Kent, "I know your business has closed, just like mine. Can you do me a big favour and stay with Carla in the new house in the Cape for a while, at least until all this virus BS is over?" he asks.

"I guess so because there is nothing I can do here. Why? What's wrong with Carla?" she asks.

"She could do with a friend right now," he replies. "Couldn't we all," Leonora sighs, "Is there more to it than the Corona virus?"

"Yes, there is, Leonora," he hesitates. "I have left Carla." "You bastard! I knew it the moment I saw you with that bitch in the club!"

"Please, Leonora, stop it: that can't be changed," he interrupts her. "Just do me a favour and go down there, I will get you a special clearance certificate and forward it to you. Thanks, Leonora, I owe you."

"You owe me shit, how could you …" but Kent has disconnected.

24 hours later, Leonora gets an e-mail confirming her special-clearance travel certificate, plus an e-mail from Susan's Travel with a flight confirmation to the Southern Cape on the following day.

"Who paid for the ticket?" she demands when she gets Susan on the line.

"Club L'Afrique, my dear," she says. "Aren't you lucky? I upgraded you to Business Class as a token of thanks for all the business you have sent my way. Will you see Carla?"

"Yes, I am going to stay with her in her new home." "Lucky you. Pity the beaches are closed. Ah well, you will just have to lie around the pool. Bye, got another call waiting."

"Bye to you, too," mutters Leonora, speed-dialling Carla's number.

"Hi, have you got a spare bed? The city is driving me crazy, Covid-Covid-Covid is all you hear from all sides. Zero event management now."

"Leonora, are you serious?!" Carla shouts, "Of course you can come. My parents are still here, but I have a king-size bed we can share. Lex can sleep on the floor."

Jeez, she forgot all about that brute of a dog. In Carla's old house the dogs were always locked away in the backyard when she visited.

"Carla," she says, panic in her voice, "you'll have to put him in the cage. You know my phobia with dogs since I was bitten by that mongrel. Dogs can smell my fear from ten metres and start growling."

"No problem, Leonora, Lex will get used to you in no time, you'll see. What time is your plane? I will come and pick you up," she says.

"Just after lunch, I think, I will phone you before I take off from here," Leonora replies.

"I am so excited. Thank you, Leonora. See you tomorrow. bye."

Don't thank me, Leonora thinks. *Thank that bloody husband of yours.*

She has known Kent for ages and never suspected a thing until she had been to Club L'Afrique one night with friends and had seen the two DJs on stage together. It had been obvious to see that more than just the music had sizzled between him and that Hot Stuff. *Jeez, I had become hot myself just watching her perform on that sound stage.*

Hm, she muses further, *he has left her. That means, she is pissed off with him. Hm, maybe I will be able to console her ... all very interesting!*

Chapter Seven

Tanya Dudnic

Not yet ready to sleep, Tanya watches the net curtains of their bedroom billow in the gentle early morning breeze.

Kent, one arm thrown over his pillow, is fast asleep beside her.

How her life has changed since her arrival in South Africa just over a year before!

After the collapse of the Soviet Union, Tanya Dudnic's parents had fled from the Ukraine and found refuge in the UK for her and her two younger brothers. While acknowledging the large Eastern European Community around London, the British government had made great efforts to integrate such a sought-after labour force.

Having no knowledge of the English language, however, her parents had obtained work in a small hotel near Oxford: her mother as a housekeeper and her father in the scullery of the hotel's kitchen. Their three children had attended a special school for Eastern European refugees where the emphasis had been on tuition in the English language and integration. The kids had battled for a while but had improved as they had progressed with their language studies.

Tanya had studied diligently, and her overall marks were above average but her performance in Gymnastics had been exceptional. Tall and slender, she still moved gracefully, and yet with feline stealth and purpose. When her teachers had suggested that she ought to attend ballet and modern dance classes, she had jumped at the opportunity, literally. A few years later she had been offered a scholarship to the London College of Dance.

She had later worked as a waitress in a pub where aspiring bands used to meet regularly to play their music, hoping to be given a break by a talent scout, like The Beatles, The Rolling Stones, and many others. With her long, auburn hair and stunning figure she had turned heads wherever she had gone. Although her passion had expressed itself in dancing, moreover, she also possessed an unusual voice, eventually being asked to join two other singers on the small stage. Before long she had found herself in recording studios, singing backing vocals for various bands and solo artists.

What fascinated her even more than the singing, once again, had been the whole recording process: the overlaying and compilations of track over track to get that ultimate sound experience. In the emerging discotheques she had seen her opportunity to combine her love of dancing and the art of mixing the music. Taking matters into her own hands, she had become the girlfriend of a DJ, and with his help she had learned the DJ trade, before leaving her by then drug- addicted mentor to run her own gigs in London.

As "DJ Hot Stuff" Tanya had become famous for her signature opening tune from the Donna Summers hit. Having then collaborated with some of the top UK pop artists, she had eventually made enough money to set out on her travels. Over the following ten years she worked in the USA, Canada, Australia, and finally in South Africa. She had not applied formally for a job at Club L'Afrique but had simply asked the resident DJ to allow her a turn. In his office at the back of the club that night Kent had heard her, took one look at her, and hired her on the spot.

She had rented a small apartment and kept pretty much to herself, but behind the mixing tables the chemistry between Kent and her had been electric. When The Rooster and Hot Stuff had mixed the tables on Friday, Saturday, and Sunday nights, the dance floor below the stage had been packed with an audience that had come to watch the DJ duo's sizzling performance, it had been fire and fury in laser motion.

Inevitably, they had ended up taking that pent-up energy to bed in her small apartment. Their first night together had caught them both by surprise: instead of the expected veracious union of bodies, their union had been tender, nearly hesitant, yet all-consuming in a way neither had experienced before. It was not just the merging of two eager bodies, but the merging of two lonely souls.

Lying in each other's arms, covered with a drenched sheet, Tanya simply spoke two words: "And now?"

Was it a one-night stand? Or dare she hope for more? "Give me time, please," Kent pleaded, "after thirty years I owe Carla more than just a messy divorce based on my adultery with you."

Adultery, is that what it was? In the eyes of society and the law, yes, but in her eyes, no. In her eyes, it was right, despite all the consequences. She wanted that man as much as he wanted her. But does he really?

After a month, Kent had bought an airy, spacious, penthouse apartment within easy commuting distance from the club, had furnished it and given her the keys to move in, saying: "It's yours, or ours, until I can make other arrangements. I have bought a property in the Cape, which I will develop for Carla. When she is settled, I will be with you for good."

She had believed him, never doubted him for a moment, even when the building project went on and on, with endless delays. She would spin her music and wait.

Now he is here for good: he had kept his word.

Carefully, she moves his hand off the pillow onto her bare hip, turning into him, she goes to sleep.

Chapter Eight

Carla & Leonora

"Oh, Leonora, it's so good of you to come. My parents are driving me crazy. This lockdown is insane, I can't get the house finished, not that I have the money, anyway. What a bloody mess!" she says in greeting, pulling Leonora to her white Mercedes Estate in the shade-cloth covered parking lot of the small, regional airport.

Talking non-stop during the nearly one-and-a-half hours' drive to her new house, Carla finally gets around to asking: "How are things with you?"

Leonora looks at her, thinking: *Do you really want to know?* But decides to excuse Carla's rudeness. *Write it down to stress. Jeez, to be dumped after over thirty years for a disc-spinning bimbo: tough for her.* She puts on a charming smile instead and says: "With the pandemic and the business closed for God-only-knows how long, we dissolved our partnership, and each decided to do our own thing of survival. "I gave up my apartment and moved back in with my mother. When the walls started closing in on me, I decided to pay you a visit, catch a bit of Cape sun. With Kent cooped up in the city, I figured you could do with some company."

She has hardly finished the sentence, when Carla blurts out: "Leonora, swear on the Bible and promise not to tell anybody, especially not my parents: Kent's not coming back."

Leonora feigns absolute shock: "What do you mean, he's not coming back?"

"Just that, he's not coming back."

"You are kidding me! Is there someone else?" Leonora asks.

"I am sure there is, but nobody is telling me a thing," says Carla, overtaking a truck in the slow lane.

Leonora thinks: *She doesn't even know about the bimbo? Is that possible, or is she in total denial?*

Driving down the steep driveway into the open triple garage, they can hear Lex barking furiously.

"I'm not getting out of the car until you have locked him away," says Leonora, crouching deep into her seat.

"All right, all right ... wait here. I'll lock him into his pen in my bedroom. He will get used to you just now. He is so sweet with my parents."

Mr Carstens comes up the stairs to the garage a few minutes later to help Leonora with her bags.

"*Boa tarde,* Leonora, you can come now," he says with a welcoming smile, showing off the few words of Portuguese he had picked up on his shopping sprees to the local vegetable farmstall. "The Brat is locked away. He is just like a naughty little boy."

"Yes," says Leonora, "only his teeth are a lot bigger and sharper."

Over dinner, the conversation is all about the virus and the Carstens being stranded here in South Africa. The parents insist that Leonora call them by their first names: Anna and Christian. "We are all cooped up together, and you are just about part of our family: we have known you for some time now."

Anna wants to go home, to be with her oldest daughter Theresa in Copenhagen but Christian is happy here with his younger daughter, who has always been the apple of his eye. "I have heard that they are going to allow senior expatriation flights soon," says Leonora. "We can phone Susan's Travel tomorrow and tell her to keep us informed."

Leonora locks herself in the guest toilet while Carla and her father transfer Lex's holding pen to the downstairs lounge. The big German Shepherd carries on as one of those caged lions you might see behind bars in a circus enclosure, except that he is barking, while growling and throwing himself against the steel bars of the pen when he sees Leonora go up the stairs to the Master bedroom.

Right away, she opens the sliding door to the balcony for some fresh sea air, and to get the dog smell out of the bedroom.

Showered and dressed in their PJs, casually stretched out on top of the king-sized bed, Carla and Leonora talk late into the night.

"This definitely beats the city," says Leonora as they turn off the lights later that night, with the sliding doors wide open, and the sound of the waves hitting the rocks at high tide.

On Carla's instruction over the next couple of days, Leonora tries to ignore Lex every time she walks past his cage, which has been set up permanently in the downstairs lounge. After two or three days, Lex has lost interest and just glares at her.

"Today I will put on his muzzle and see how we get on," says Carla. To Leonora's surprise, the big dog is calm, listening to Carla's sharp command of "Leave". But the moment Leonora gets too close to Lex, he gives her a sharp head-butt with his muzzle.

After a couple of days, Leonora's thighs are covered with bruises. In utter frustration, she resorts to wearing jeans instead of skimpy shorts: not what she really wanted out of a holiday at the seaside.

Eventually, three weeks later, when Anna's wailing reaches fever pitch, that she must go home, Susan confirms an expatriation flight at astronomical prices.

"What can we do?" says Christian. "We must go. We don't know how long this will go on for."

Although she does not show it openly Leonora is most relieved at Anna's and Christian's departure. Now she can move into the vacated guest room and out of Carla's king-size bed. She had reached the end of her self-control and had been close to giving in.

Slowly, take your time ...

With the parents gone, Carla and Leonora quickly settle into a working routine. By the time the lockdown has been relaxed and the beaches have been opened again, they even begin to enjoy themselves socially.

Leonora has started selling a range of exclusive South African beauty products online, mainly to the USA, and is very busy at the weirdest times, due to the differing time zones.

Carla has set up her weight-lifting equipment at the side of the house, close to the swimming pool and trains daily to keep in shape while the gyms are still closed.

Kent releases funds to finish the house. At long last, the curtains are put up in the bedrooms and the property is fenced so that Lex can now be let out without fear for the neighbour's safety. The Malawian gardener who comes once a week simply ignores Lex and is, in turn, ignored by Lex.

Life just about returns to some sort of normality but for how long? Nobody knows.

"Carla, is that you?" shrieks a middle-aged, going-to-flab guy, getting up from his towel, spread out in the sand of Central Beach.

"Chris? These bloody masks! One can't recognise anybody!" says Carla.

"I'd recognise that body if it was lined up with a hundred others," he beams.

"Big deal," she says, self-consciously pulling her sarong around herself.

"Chris, what are you doing here?" she says and, turning to Leonora, she adds: "Leonora, meet Chris, the Number One Kérastase product agent."

"Hi," says Leonora, her half-smile hidden behind the mask.

"I am on lockdown holiday," says Chris. "I have an apartment down here. You must come for dinner, both of you. I wondered what happened to you after you sold your salon. We must catch up. What is your number? I'll send you the directions to my place: it's not far from here. Are we on?" he says.

Carla looks at Leonora, who shrugs and nods. Carla gets her phone out, scrolls through her contacts, and dials his number. His phone rings from his bag on the towel.

"Still got you in my contacts," she winks at him.

"Oh, darling, you make me blush," he says. "Come at six: we have a splendid view of the sunset."

He prattles on incessantly, until Leonora finally chips in. "I need a pee. Let's go." They bump elbows and leave Chris hooting with laughter. "See you later, darlings."

"He's too gay," says Leonora as soon as they are out of earshot, "totally over the top."

"He used to be a mediocre hairdresser before he became a rep," Carla responds. "He is good at that, and harmless. Apart from that, the crowd he mixes with are good fun. We had some really hilarious parties over the years," she assures Leonora.

Half an hour later, they are standing with two coffees-to-go in the entrance of a small supermarket.

"Leonora? Good afternoon," says a well-groomed, silver-haired man, stopping right in front of them.

"Mr van der Walt? I am sorry, I did not recognise you behind your mask," she says, stretching out her clenched fist for a knuckle bump.

"Elbows will have to do, my dear," he says. "Liz is still talking about you. How you excelled in organising our surprise golden-wedding anniversary affair at the Shamwari Game Ranch."

"Well thank you Mr van der Walt," says Leonora. "I am glad, since my job is precisely to organise memorable events."

"I know, I know," he says, "but you truly excelled, the attention to detail. Are you down here for long?"

"Hard to say in these uncertain times, but I guess so. I am staying with my best friend Carla in her new home," she says, pulling Carla closer to them.

He pulls out his phone and quickly scrolls through the contacts. "Here you are," he says, "is the number still the same?"

"Still the same," she says.

"We will call you: the two of you must come for cocktails," he says, "Liz would love to see you again." With a glance at his Rolex he says, "You will have to excuse me: I just came for some capers to finish off a salmon dish that I am preparing for later on. See you soon." They wave a goodbye to his back.

"We must stop going out," says Carla, "two invites in one outing."

She does not realise how true her statement is. Starting with Chris's dinner party that night, Carla and Leonora are constantly invited, every time meeting more old acquaintances, and making new ones.

Life is getting hectic.

"Poor Lex, I am feeling guilty leaving him alone so much now," Carla says.

"But he sleeps at night," says Leonora, rubbing the bruises on her thighs.

A few days later, the heavens open and the long-awaited rains come down heavily for the first time since the construction of the house had been completed.

All through the night and the following day, over 100 mm come down. The rain cascades down the retaining wall at the back, eroding a deep channel at its base. The pool overflows and is filled with mud from the rear of the garden. The lawn created on top of the excavated and compacted material looks like a landscape from the moon, with deep craters and cracks.

All that is nothing compared to what happens inside the house. Normally covered with an iron grid, the water channel in front of the triple garage overflows. It simply cannot cope with the quantity and velocity of water coming down the steep driveway. The garage, which is on the third floor of the house, gets flooded. From there the water runs down the interior stairs into the Master bed- and bathroom on the second floor, out from under the sliding doors to the balcony, and cascades onto the veranda, where it joins the water coming from inside. The stream inside in the meantime has continued down the stairs through the guest bed- and bathroom, on down to the living-room, the kitchen, Carla's office, and guest toilet, to flow, by now much slower, out of the sliding-glass doors, over the veranda and, into the overflowing pool. It's a complete nightmare.

"Kent!" Carla screams into her phone hysterically, while Lex jumps from the settee into the water and back onto the settee, and Leonora is salvaging their personal belongings that have been submerged in their bedrooms.

"Kent! The fucking house is under water! We are going to float into the valley below and then into the fucking ocean!"

"Calm down, Carla ..." he murmurs.

"Where the fuck are you?" Carla interrupts him. "Curled up with a girlfriend, nice and snug in a warm bed?"

Did Leonora tell her about Tanya? he wonders. "Listen up for a moment!" he shouts to make himself heard over her tirade of expletives. "I will phone the architect and the contractor to come and do an inspection and remedy the situation."

"Remedy the situation?" she mimics him; tossing the phone onto the kitchen counter, from where it slides off and onto the flooded kitchen floor. "SHIT!!!" she screams and dives after it, before wrapping it in a dishcloth.

Chapter Nine

Kent

"Thomas, good morning," says Kent to the CEO of Fowler's property management company. "How is the transfer of my Cape house into Carla's name progressing?"

"Hi, Kent. Should be through any day now. How is the Northcliff Penthouse? Are you enjoying the views?" asks Thomas.

"It's absolutely stunning," says Kent. "Sunrise over the whole of Jo'burg and sunset from the top of the cliff as far as the eye can see. Great architecture, the way they nestled the building into the cliff; eight floors facing east to the city, and only four floors above the summit. It's great, a superb find, Thomas, thanks again. Sorry got to make some urgent calls ... Text me when the transfer is through, please. Bye."

Cutting the call to Thomas, he speed dials the architect of the Cape house ... No reply, straight to voice mail.

"Eric, it's Kent, please give me a call. It's urgent."

Bastard, took his fee and when the shit hits the fan, he's disappeared, thinks Kent and speed dials Hennie de Bruyn, the earthwork contractor's number.

"Hennie, good day. How can I help you, Mister Fowler? Have you all settled in?"

"Hennie, no I have not. I am back up in the city. Carla tells me you had a lot of rain."

"Mister Fowler, it bucketed down; more than 100 millimetres in 24 hours. My smallholding on the river is totally under water and I spent most of the night moving my livestock onto higher ground ..."

"Your smallholding is not the only thing under water; my wi- ... er ... Carla tells me the house is floating into the ocean, and the pool is full of mud. Will you please go out there and see what needs doing? I'll send the insurance assessor out to write up the claim.

"Hello? Are you still there?" *Bloody phone!*

"Mister Fowler? Sorry, I lost you there. I was going to assure you that I will go to your house immediately."

"Thanks, Hennie. Send me some pictures and give me a plan of action, please," says Kent.

Then he speed-dials his lawyer. "Ron – Kent. Can I come and see you about a divorce? ... Yes, my divorce ... Tomorrow, 10 o'clock is fine. Thanks, see you."

Who next? he thinks, when two soft hands pull him back into his recliner. "Divorce?" says Tanya, massaging his neck gently.

"Yes, I have heard enough of her profanities. I want her out of my life, once and for all," he says.

"Adultery?" she asks, "that could become nasty."

"No, I am going to offer her the Cape house, plus whatever alimony the lawyer feels is commensurate."

"Sounds fair. How will you find out if she will accept or launch a counter claim?"

"I'll have inside information," and he tells Tanya about Leonora.

"Can you trust her?"

"Trust her? Hah! Wait and see Ms Leonora is going to spit poison just now."

Tanya gives Kent a quizzical look. *Has this man got a dark side she does not know about?*

Chapter Ten

Hennie de Bruyn

Rubbing his chin thoughtfully, Hennie remembers the Fowler contract well. It had started off as a straightforward excavation job, cutting into the slope and balancing the cut by spreading the soil on the site to accommodate the footprint of the house. On one of their earlier visits, the Fowlers had inspected the staked-out area where the foundations were to be dug and had argued with the architect that the living area would be far too small.

The revised plans had then made it necessary to excavate much deeper. The extra soil that consequently had been dug out of the upper slope had to be carted away, as they had no more space on the site. A much higher retaining wall had been needed also and the garage level had to be raised one more floor, otherwise it would have been impossible to get a car down there. Even with the extra level the driveway had remained very steep.

Hennie did not complain because a relatively normal job had virtually tripled in size for him. *Their change of design meant much more money for me, thank you very much.*

This morning, Hennie also remembered that the couple were arrogant and she, a real looker, had been particularly demanding. He grabbed his rain jacket and got into his pick-up. "Let's have a look-see," he muttered as he drove down his bumpy farm driveway.

Fifteen minutes later, he stands at the top of the Fowlers' steep driveway.

My, my, he thinks, *the stormwater has overflown the service road gutter. That one is for the developers to sort out.*

The loud barking of what sounds like, a big, vicious dog, makes him hesitate at the open garage door.

"Lex!" Hennie hears a commanding, female voice. *"Platz!* In your room!"

"Are you the contractor?" A slim female, clad in skimpy cut-off jeans and long, brown hair, asks him.

That's not Mrs Fowler, he thinks, *but wow, what a beauty, who is she?*

As if sensing his question, she says: "I am Leonora, Carla's friend. You can come in. Carla is just putting the dog away."

"I am okay with dogs," he says. "I have a few mutts myself on the farm."

"You are not okay with Lex, trust me," says Leonora.

At that moment a dishevelled Mrs Fowler, also in skimpy, cut-off jeans, appears.

Look at that! he gapes. "Mrs Fowler ...?" he starts.

"Call me Carla," she says. "Come in and look at the bloody mess."

She is right, it is a bloody mess. "Please phone the local office of your insurers to come and make an assessment," Hennie says. "In the meantime, I will take pictures and make notes. Tomorrow I will bring a team of workers to help with the clean-up. By the way, my name is Hennie," he says, smiling at the two women reassuringly.

"Thanks Hennie," Carla says, do you mind talking to my husband if I get him on the phone?"

"Not at all," he says, taking the phone from her a moment later.

"Hello, Mr Fowler," he says and relates what he has been able to see so far, and what should be done.

"Now," says Fowler, "the insurance may be a bit of a problem. I am not sure if we are covered for floods, with the house being on top of the ridge. I will have to check."

Over the next two weeks, Hennie works hard with his team. The insurance assessor has confirmed that they are covered, and they have agreed to an amount for fixing the damage. That said, there are a lot of areas that are not covered, like the muddy pool, the sink-holes in the lawn, and so on but Hennie has his team there, and pushes them to do far more than what the insurers have agreed to pay.

He feels sorry for Carla, since he has gotten to know quite a bit about her during their tea and lunch breaks together. The other girl, Leonora, keeps pretty much to herself, always busy on her phone or the computer. But Carla is around non-stop. She can't believe that Hennie has even made friends with Lex and plays with him, although the dog remains muzzled.

One lunchtime, she bursts out: "Things were just going nicely; the two of us were invited out a lot and met loads of nice people. Now this mess has cooped us up; too much to do to get a chance to relax."

"There is a live band playing in a new restaurant not far from my farm, why don't the three of us try it out tonight?" he says.

"The three of us? You mean you and your wife and I?" Carla says.

"No, I am single. I mean you and Leonora and myself," he responds.

"Leonora will not come. She is working on a big order and the evenings are the only time she can get them online, so it will just be the two of us," she replies.

"All right," Hennie grins, "then I will come for you at half-past-seven, after I have fed the animals and cleaned myself up."

Carla likes that grin of his. *It makes him look younger than his fifty-two years,* she thinks. *Oh well, let's see what he is like away from work.*

Hennie rushes through his chores; showers, decides to have another shave, and puts on a fresh pair of jeans, a checked long-sleeved shirt, and tan loafers. This is the first time he feels so good since Katy passed away.

The restaurant is a converted barn with both indoor and outdoor seating areas, a bar, and a small dance floor in front of an equally small, raised stage. On the far side there is a pizza oven and an open-plan kitchen.

The whole place is filled with pot plants and hanging plants, suggesting an outdoor atmosphere, as well as providing some privacy to the clusters of small and large tables, or settees with low tables before them.

"Hi, I am Gary," says a slim blond man in his late thirties. "Welcome. You are Hennie, right? Aren't you from the farm down the road?"

"Yes, that's right," Hennie replies. I watched you put this place together. Great job. Meet Carla. We came to hear the music, maybe chew on a pizza."

"Hi Carla," says Gary. "Good to see you both. Make yourselves at home." He turns to greet the next group arriving.

They find a settee with a view of the stage where the band is busy setting up.

"Drink?" Hennie asks her when a waiter comes to their table.

"Gin and pink tonic in a tall glass, with lots of ice," says Carla.

"Light beer for me please," Hennie orders.

The moment the band starts up, conversation becomes difficult. The band is feeling its way, judging by the near capacity crowd. Tunes from the 80s and 90s get the first couples onto the floor. Hennie gestures to the dance floor and gets up.

Although it has been a long time since she danced in public, Carla is into her second, tall, pink gin, which helps to overcome her inhibition, They start off all clumsy, self-conscious, both obviously out of practice. Hennie is no John Travolta or Patrick Swayze, but he gets along.

"Enough," says Carla after five or six dances in a row. "I need a drink."

With a fresh round of drinks in their hands, they find a settee outside in the cooler garden area, away from the increasing volume of the music and shrieks of laughter coming from one of the long tables occupied by girls in their twenties, apparently a hens' party.

It's amazing what a bit of alcohol does to an individual's behaviour, Hennie thinks.

To Carla, Hennie seems relaxed and easy to talk to. Away from his workers he loses his bossy manner, displaying a quick, keen sense of humour. Carla is surprised by the way he listens to her every word attentively, as if he is in awe of her. *Of course,* she realises, *I am the wife of his multi-millionaire client. In fact, strictly speaking, I am also his client.*

After another round, Carla does not know if the drinks are loosening her tongue, but – all of a sudden – she has an urge to confide in Hennie.

"Kent has left me!" she blurts out, tears of rage welling up in her eyes. "He went up to the city, to look after our business, but told me that he won't be back. I can't prove it, but I suspected for some time, that he is involved with someone else."

Hennie feels very uncomfortable. *What am I supposed to say or do?* Before he can think any further, however, she solves his dilemma by turning into him, burying her head in his shoulder, and sobbing.

"Thirty-two years! After thirty-two years, the bastard leaves me."

All Hennie can do is hold her and comfort her.

"Sorry, Hennie," she says, "you are the only person to know, other than Leonora. I just had to get it out."

"It's okay, Carla," he replies. "I understand the pain and the rage. I felt the same when the cancer took Katy from me. Why me? Why us? Let me pay and take you home: it's getting late, and Leonora and Lex will worry about you."

From that evening on, their relationship changes. Although the bulk of the work has been done, Hennie starts to take a closer look, beyond his contractual commitment, at the house, and especially the garden. He now understands that she is actually on a very tight budget. Her husband only sends her money for absolute necessities, which, he guesses, is not a lot. The perks are the house, the car, and the utility payments. On spare days, when he has nothing else to do, Hennie gets his staff to thin out some plants from his farm and plant them in her garden. He makes himself useful in the house: fixing pictures, bathroom towel rails, and toilet-roll holders.

"Is he just your handyman?" Leonora teases Carla one evening when Hennie has left, after having eaten with them. She is not amused by "this guy" sticking around more and more and coming between the two friends. She excuses herself under the pretext of having work to do, and escapes to her bedroom. The most relaxed is Lex, who now rests his chin on Hennie's knee, whenever he sits down.

It is Leonora's decision that she needs to go to Cape Town on business, however, that seems to seal the affair between Hennie and Carla. On her return a week later, it is obvious that the two are sleeping together and making no bones about it.

Leonora has nowhere else to go, other than her mother, so she bites her tongue and pretends to accept the situation as perfectly normal. *Let's see how long this will last.*

"Hi, Leonora," she hears Kent's familiar voice on the phone late one night, "is the house in good order again? Is Carla alright?"

"Do you actually care?" Leonora hisses. "To tell you the truth; she is over you. The contractor has fixed more than just the house." Immediately regretting her outburst, she breaks the connection. *How long must I still put up with this mess?* Carla and Hennie go out to parties with his friends, sometimes the three of them go out together, and sometimes Leonora is invited out by her friends.

It seems to work, thinks Carla, accepting the way things are.

Hennie has got a boat on the river in which the three of them go on picnics upstream, spending the day on one of the many protruding sandbanks, sunbathing, swimming in the clear, fresh water.

It is an ideal way to forget about the worries of the world. Carla can feel herself relax and looks forward to spending time with Hennie. The feeling is mutual, and their relationship takes its natural course.

One night, it may have been after two a.m., Leonora is jerked out of a deep sleep by Carla's screams.

"Leonora, help me! Help me! Call an ambulance! Hurry! It's Hennie, please hurry!"

Leonora reacts immediately, makes the call, then runs through to the master bedroom. She finds Carla, dressed in her PJs, holding a pale Hennie, clad in PJ shorts, in her arms. "He is dying. He is having a heart attack. Oh my God, what can I do?"

Leonora is stunned: she is not a medical expert, but she can see that any effort is too late.

"Put Lex away," she says to Carla. "I will go upstairs and open up for the ambulance." She remembers to phone the estate's security officer, to alert them of the coming ambulance.

Lights flashing, the ambulance comes to a halt at the top of the steep driveway, while two paramedics rush towards her, "One floor down, open door on the left," points Leonora.

"He woke me, saying he was not feeling well," Carla cries, "then he had convulsions, I held him. Then he went all quiet, too quiet, he must have passed away in my arms."

The Medics confirm that there is nothing they can do for him. Understandably Carla goes into shock. She refuses to eat or leave the house to walk Lex. It is Leonora who holds things together.

"Carla? Oh, hi, Leonora," she hears Kent's familiar voice when she answers Carla's phone one afternoon, "maybe you can help me; any idea where that contractor Hennie de Bruyn is? I need his final invoice to close off the insurance claim."

Jeez, what must I tell him? "No idea Kent," she decides to reply, then unable to deceive him, she blurts out: "He died of a heart attack a week ago."

"Oh no, that's terrible. I heard from mutual acquaintances we made down there, that he and Carla were spending time together: eating out, going to parties ... you must have known about it?"

"Yes I did, Kent, so what? You aren't exactly living like a monk, are you?" Leonora flares.

"Hold it, Leonora, I wasn't accusing her, just stating facts. Can I speak to Carla now?"

"Kent, I am sorry: she asked me not to disturb her."

"I see," he says, "ask her to give me a call, please."

Shit, how did I get into the middle of this mess? Leonora thinks.

CHAPTER ELEVEN

KENT

"Good morning, Kent," says Thomas cheerfully. "I have just received the transfer papers for the Cape house, you want me to courier then down to Carla for signatures?"

"Morning, Thomas," Kent replies, "How would you and your missus like a couple of days in the Cape sunshine? Apart from Carla's signatures, there is the matter of the final bill from the contractor who handled all the storm damage repairs. Only problem is that he had a heart attack and passed away."

"Thanks, Kent, we'd appreciate getting out of the city for a couple of days now that the level has been lifted a notch," says Thomas. "I have the file right here with the transfer documents, I'll handle it, and see what I can sort out for the outstanding invoice. Chat to you soon. Bye."

Kent has not even put his phone back in his pocket when it crows again. Checking the caller ID, he answers: "Morning Dad, what's up?"

Without greeting, Graham says: "I just got a call from the liquor squad. They informed me that they caught some looters in the store that is part of the night club. Problem is, they say, that the leader of the looters, apparently a giant of a man, had the store keys in his pocket."

"A-a-and," says Kent, dragging the word out.

"They finally got his name out of one of his accomplices: his name is ..."

"Bobby Ncobo," Kent finishes for him.

"Right on the mark, son," says Graham Fowler. "How long do you think it will take for them to put you and Bobby together?"

At that moment, Tanya comes rushing through from the study, waving her own phone urgently at Kent. "Dumi," she mouths.

"Hang on a moment, Dad, I'll put us on conference with Dumi ... Yes, Dumi?"

"Kent, the cops followed one of the looters' *bakkies* to a shebeen they were delivering to. There was a shootout. Then a fire started inside the shebeen. Instead of calling the fire brigade, they let it burn down. Kent, there were people inside; Kent, the Shebeen queen was inside. Kent, it was Bobby's wife, it was her shebeen ..." The rest is lost in terrible sobs.

Kent gives the phone to Tanya. "Please, talk to him, calm him down."

Returning to his own call, he cancels the conference connection, and says: "Dad, are you there?"

"Yes," rasps his father, "even after over 40 years in the country I can't get used to the African way of justice."

"Dad," says Kent. "We must get out of this business."

"We won't find buyers now. Who wants to buy bottle stores if they can't sell booze?"

"Then we have to liquidate!"

"Have you ever heard of a bottle store being liquidated?" snorts his father.

"I don't know, Dad, but I have had it," says Kent, as he hears a loud knock on the penthouse door.

Chapter Twelve

Carla

Carla lies curled up next to Lex on her rumpled king-size bed when Leonora resolutely pushes open the bedroom door. Close to gagging, she finds a place for the tray she brought with her on the dressing table. Lex stares at her as docile as a lamb, tail whacking the sheet in greeting.

"I brought you some coffee and muesli with almond milk," Leonora says. "Please eat something: you are fading away."

As Leonora goes to open the sliding door behind the closed curtains, Carla croaks at her: "Go away, leave me alone!"

Overcoming her urge to vomit, Leonora says: "Carla, it's enough now. Stop blaming yourself. It's not your fault Hennie had a heart attack. You heard what the doctor said: he had a heart condition."

"Yes, but the sex ..." Carla trails off bursting into tears again.

"That's rubbish and you know it," snaps Leonora. "You were sleeping."

To her surprise, Lex follows her out of the bedroom, down the stairs, and goes through the wide-open doors into the garden.

Not five minutes later, Carla comes down the stairs, carrying the tray Leonora had taken up to her. "Thank you, Leonora," she says, placing the empty cup and breakfast bowl into the dishwasher. Dabbing her eyes, swollen from crying, she flops down on the settee next to Leonora. "Why is all this happening to me? This was supposed to be my dream come true, but it turned into an absolute nightmare: Kent leaving me after thirty-two years of marriage, the flood, then Hennie ..." She breaks into a fresh stream of tears, as Leonora gently pulls her friend into her arms.

Is this what I've been waiting for? No not like this: I can't take advantage of this vulnerable woman now. Leonora jumps up and says: "Why don't we take Lex to the beach? We'll take the muzzle and harness, and keep to the right, toward the rocks, where there are only a few people."

A glitter of light appears in Carla's eyes. "Yes, let's try it," she says with a hesitant look.

Seeing the muzzle and harness, Lex cowers down as if to say *I have not done anything.* Involuntarily, Carla laughs for the first time in days: "It's okay, Lexie," she says. "We are not putting you away; we are going walkies."

Hearing that magic word, the big dog jumps up and dashes upstairs to sit expectantly next to the Mercedes Estate car. Clad in bikinis, sarongs, sandals, and wide-brimmed sunhats the two women join him a few minutes later.

They are on the return leg along the water's edge when Carla's phone buzzes. Letting it go to voice message, she listens to an only vaguely familiar voice. "Hi Carla, it's Thomas Banks from property management, please give me a call."

Thomas? I wonder what he wants, she thinks.

"That's all I need," she says to Leonora, "Maybe Kent wants me out of HIS house, and wants to offer me some pay-off, or apartment. Well, he can go and jump. All my hard-earned money went into this project."

She pushes the redial button. "Thomas, how are you?" Not waiting for a reply, she continues: "What can I do for you?"

"Hello Carla, are you well? I need you to sign some papers for me."

"Thomas, I am not in Jo'burg, I am in the Cape."

"So am I. In fact, my hired car is parked at the top of your driveway."

"Oh wow! Give me fifteen minutes max," says Carla. "Maybe have a coffee at the supermarket down the road."

"It's alright. I'll just wait here. It's not every day I get to see a view like this," Thomas replies.

Twenty minutes later, they are sitting under the sun umbrella on the veranda, overlooking the pool, the garden, and the blue waters of the bay below.

"This is nice," says Thomas looking around. Leonora sets a tall pitcher of iced tea and glasses in front of them and excuses herself. Taking an appreciative sip of the beverage, Thomas opens a briefcase and extracts two Manila folders. Carla is watching him wearily, not certain what this is all about. "Kent will have told you ..."

She interrupts Thomas sharply. "He does not tell me anything."

"I see," says Thomas, not surprised by the bitterness in the tone of her voice. He pulls a sheaf of papers out of the uppermost folder. "These are the papers transferring this property into your name," he says. " I need you to sign."

"What? Did I hear you right? This is now my house, my property?"

"Yes, that's what Kent wants," says Thomas, as Carla exhales a painful groan.

"So that's it then, isn't it? The point of no return."

"Sorry, Carla," mumbles Thomas, indicating where she has to sign.

A couple of minutes later, with all pages signed, he leaves her a copy, assuring her that the property deeds will be issued shortly.

Then he turns his attention to the second folder. "This is the paperwork for the insurance claim concerning the flood damage you incurred. Did you claim for personal damages from your household insurance?" When she nods, he continues: "I believe that contractor de Bruyn died of a heart attack shortly after completion of the work. We need the final invoice that his Estate can be paid. Would you perhaps know who took over the business, or who are his next of kin?" Thomas says, looking up from the folder in front of him, to see Carla ashen faced, fighting to control her tears.

"I have no idea," says Carla before changing her mind saying: "I believe an older sister is now on the farm. I don't really know; I just recall extending condolences to the family after the funeral service."

"I see," says Thomas. "Do you know where the farm is?"

"It's on the river a couple of kilometres out of town. It's signposted; you can't miss it," says Carla, seeing him through the house and up the steep driveway.

"Leonora, Leonora!" Carla shouts, letting Lex out of his pen in the bedroom.

"Yes Carla?"

"He transferred the house into my name," Carla says, waving the copies at her friend.

Leonora rushes over and takes Carla into a tight embrace. "I am so happy for you. Everything will be alright, after all."

Carla extricates herself from the rather overwhelming embrace and says: "Do you want to move in with me? I mean, for a while, until things return to normal, and you can get back to your event planning?"

"Well, I am sort of here already, aren't I? We may as well make it official."

"Sounds like we are coming out of the closet, the way you say *make it official*," says Carla, giving her friend a meaningful look.

Leonora turns away quickly, hiding the deep blush in her face. Changing the subject, she composes herself and says: "Come let's go out and celebrate tonight: my treat."

As usual, their plan of a quiet meal is changed as they walk into the restaurant: "Hey, Carla, Leonora, come join us," urges Chris, rushing over to greet them.

Chapter Thirteen

Kent

Responding to the repeated sharp raps on the apartment door, Tanya looks through the spyhole to see two men in plain clothes staring at the door impatiently.

"Yes?" she calls out. "Police. Open up."

"How do I know that?" Tanya replies with a strong Australian accent, while she hears Kent's phone crowing behind her.

"Can you hold up some kind of ID, please?" she says.

A hand holding a police ID, appears within the lens. Leaving the security chain on, she inches the door open. "What can I do for you?" Tanya says firmly, as Kent moves her gently out of the way; closes the door sufficiently to unlatch the security chain, before opening the door wide.

"Gentlemen, come in," he says. "What can I do for you?"

"Mr Kent Fowler?" asks the taller of the two plain-clothed policemen.

"Yes, sir," says Kent.

"You need to come with us to police headquarters. Captain Moerane has some questions for you."

"Is that where you have taken my father?" asks Kent, adding, "that was my mother on the phone just now: she is beside herself with worry."

"I am afraid that can't be helped," says the taller of the two, while the shorter, stockier policeman pulls out a pair of handcuffs.

"Are you coming on your own accord, or do I need to cuff you?" he demands.

"That won't be necessary," Kent replies. "Let's go."

Tanya calls out to him: "I'll phone Ron and go to your mother."

"Thanks," says Kent over his shoulder, "but she may not want to see you. She is very fond of Carla, despite ..." the rest is lost as the elevator door closes behind the three men.

Tanya picks up Kent's phone from the small table next to his recliner. *Good thinking, Kent. The cops would have taken it off you to scan your contacts,* she thinks. *What's the lawyer's name again? Ron ... Here we are: Ron Edwards.* She speed-dials the number.

"Swart & Edwards, how may I help you?" a secretary answers the phone.

"Mr. Edwards please, it is urgent," says Tanya.

"Who is calling?" asks the secretary.

"It's Mrs Pope from the Vatican! Does it matter to you who your boss talks to, or are you just nosy?"

There is a click and then: "Ron Edwards, how can I help you?"

"Hi, this is Tanya 'Hot Stuff', the Adulteress in Kent Fowler's divorce action ..."

Ron's laughter interrupts her: "Slow down, Tanya, there is no adulteress in Kent's divorce. Kent and Carla are evenly matched: one each at the moment, so we won't go that route. But you did not phone me to discuss Kent's divorce or your alleged adultery. Give me the real reason for your call."

"Kent's in trouble with the police, or more accurately, the Liquor Squad ..." She stops when she hears him whistle through his teeth.

"You don't have to say any more: where is he?"

"They took him to headquarters where a Captain Moerane wants to ask some questions. They left less than five minutes ago."

"I am not a criminal lawyer, but I'll go down there with my partner Kallie Swart, he is the right man for the job. Leave it with me."

"Mr Edwards, I think you will find Kent and his father at police headquarters."

"Oops, that sounds serious, I better get going. I'll phone you later ..."

"Mr Edwards ..."

"Yes?"

"Just so that you know, bail is no problem, my piggybank holds more dollars than Fort Knox."

Ron laughs and disconnects.

In the meantime, Kent is being escorted from the underground parking into an elevator that takes them up to the fourth floor. He sees his father seated on a wooden bench at the far end of the corridor. "Bobby!" is all he says when Kent sits down next to him.

"Have you seen him?" Kent asks.

"No, he is locked up downstairs somewhere."

Just then the door next to them opens and a police officer says: "Come in. Captain Moerane will see you now."

The Captain motions Kent and his father to two chairs facing his desk. "We need some explanations from you about Fowler's liquor stores, and the store beneath the nightclub in particular. We now know that the stores warehouse doors were opened by the nightclub manager Robert Ncobo and that he personally loaded the *bakkie* with two of your nightclub staff. Is it common practice that your managers can help themselves to liquor from your warehouses?"

Kent sits further forward on his straight-backed chair, and says: "Captain Moerane, for the record, my father is Chairman of the Board, and no longer actively involved in the day-to-day running of the business. I am the CEO of Fowler's Liquor Emporium and the L'Afrique Nightclub.

"With regards to Robert Ncobo possessing keys to the warehouse, I can explain that. The property houses three operations: the liquor store and warehouse on the ground floor; the cocktail bar and restaurant on the first floor; and the night club on the second and third floors. The cocktail bar and the club, of which Bobby is the manager, draw stocks with an in-house transfer from the warehouse."

"That is not my concern," says Moerane. "How *you* move your stock within the building is your problem. How the liquor moves *out* of that building is my concern. The liquor store has set *regulated* selling times. Your bar and club have a licence for liquor consumption inside the building. In other, simpler terms: liquor can only leave the building *inside a person's stomach,* not in the back of a bakkie. Whether Mr Ncobo is stealing from you or selling it on your behalf, is unlawful. You understand what I am getting at? If he is stealing, you need to press charges. If he is selling with your consent, in contravention of the President's decree, it puts you both in deep trouble. What is it going to be?"

Before Kent has a chance to reply, his father intervenes: "A couple of days ago, after the announcement, I called a special management meeting, explaining our financial situation, and giving strict instructions for adherence to the law in lockdown."

"I am glad to hear it," says the Captain, "now it remains for me to decide whether Ncobo acted on his own accord, or if he was in cahoots with your son."

Kent blanches, totally caught off guard by that remark. He had just contemplated asking Moerane what he knew about what had happened at the Shebeen, but now bites his tongue, and decides not to divulge what he has been told by Dumisani.

Captain Moerane then turns to Fowler senior: "You can go home now: just keep yourself available for further questioning once we have interviewed your store managers. As for you," he turns to Kent, "we will keep you with us for further questioning when my investigators have finished taking statements from all those we arrested in your warehouse and at the Shebeen."

The stocky plain-clothed policeman steps forward and motions Kent to follow him to the charge office. Before locking Kent into a holding cell, he relieves him of his watch, his wallet, and the belt of his jeans.

Meanwhile, the two lawyers Swart and Edwards are in the ground-floor reception area trying to ascertain the whereabouts of their clients but without much success. It is only when Graham Fowler walks through on his way out that they hear what is going on. "Captain Moerane is the investigating officer. You need to see him to get to Kent, Bobby, and whoever else they are holding," says the distraught Graham.

"Let me take you home," offers Ron, "Kallie can handle this on his own."

Chapter Fourteen

Carla

Leonora now spends as much time with Carla as her busy schedule permits and life seems to return to "pre-Hennie" days for the three of them. They take long walks on the beach with Lex, followed by a swim in their crystal-clear pool. While Leonora attends to her on-line cosmetics sales, Carla gets back into weight- and heavy-lift training.

Maybe a year after Kent and Carla were married, they had decided to join the local gym. Initially, they had trained together but as Kent's time was taken up more and more by the liquor-store expansions, she took to training by herself. Well, not strictly speaking by herself, but without Kent.

She was drawn to leg exercises, as her arms were tired in the evening from cutting and especially blow-drying hair for ten hours a day. With her strong legs, she attempted squats with ever-increasing weights. Soon Carla had found herself training among the heavyweights of the gym: the hardcore "steroid strutters" who had experienced difficulties in getting out of their singlet vests.

Of course, when younger men grow these monstrous muscles, their tattoos were inevitable. One guy with an amazingly sculpted torso had displayed a cobra's head tattoo on his back; others were adorned with tattoos on their arms or legs. To this day, Carla was not sure what had made her have her own tattoo done: a rare blue butterfly, low on her back just above her bikini line. Maybe it had been inspired by Kent's trademark rooster on the bicep of his left arm.

Given that his dream had always been to launch Club L'Afrique, she had attended the opening party, but had never gone again. It had always been Kent's domain, just as her hairdressing salon had been her own. When both of them had gained celebrity status – Kent the renowned DJ Rooster; she the world champion hairdresser – it had become harder and harder for them to leave their egos at the door.

And then came the German Shepherds for security reasons

and companionship in those long, lonely nights. Although she received many invitations to parties or restaurant outings, Carla had stayed home, using her two dogs as an excuse.

Over the years, she had owned several generations of German Shepherds. Now she is down to one: her Lex, the most protective and precious of them all. He had found his way into the centre of her heart and her king-size bed, pushing Kent to one side on the rare occasions he slept at home.

"Lex is not himself," Carla says to Leonora one day on their way back from a walk on the beach.

"How old is he now?" Leonora responds.

"Wait, let me think ... He was born on 2012, or was it 2013? How time flies! He must be ten," Carla confirms.

When she takes the dog to a vet a couple of days later, he checks Lex over and says with a rueful smile: "I am afraid it happens to all of us: old age. It claims the strongest of us eventually."

"How long has he got?" Carla asks, tears welling up in her eyes.

"Hard to say in a big dog like that: six months, maybe less. It's the back legs or the hips that give in. Don't walk him too hard and give him these vitamins to strengthen him."

"Carla! Carla!" Leonora shouts, motioning Carla to take out the earbuds of her phone.

Dumping the heavy set of weights onto the mat in front of her, Carla pulls out the buds. "What?" she manages, wiping the perspiration from her brow.

"There is a guy at the door who says he is a messenger of the court."

"What now?" says Carla, taking two steps at a time to get to the small side gate next to the garage.

"Mrs Fowler?" asks a middle-aged man dressed in a suit and tie.

"That's me," Carla replies. "Aren't you hot in that suit in this weather? Come inside."

The messenger of the court, obviously embarrassed, stares at Carla's scanty gym slip. Looking up into Carla's face, he says: "May I see some type of ID please?"

"Sure, are you going to come in or wait out here?"

"I will just wait here for you if you don't mind. I have a busy day today."

Five minutes later, she has presented her ID, signed for the document, and is on her way back into the house. Slitting the A4 envelope open with a kitchen knife, she pulls out its contents: *Divorce documents, is that possible?*

The finality hits her like a punch in the gut.

As she sinks onto the settee to study the document, Leonora sits down beside her. "Leonora, please, can you read this to me, my hands are shaking too much."

Used to reading contracts and their fine print from her event-planning days, where everything is recorded in minuscule detail, she flips through the pages, muttering as she goes. "Grounds for divorce: irreconcilable breakdown of the marriage ... blah, blah, blah ... amicable settlement ... blah, blah, what? Jeez, Carla, is this guy for real? Look at the alimony he is offering you ..."

Carla snatches the papers out of Leonora's hands and starts to read from the beginning. As she reads, she is forced to stop repeatedly to wipe the tears from her eyes. "Oh, Kent ..." she utters time and again. Finally, she pushes the document back into the brown A4 envelope and reaches for her phone. Speed dialling Kent's number, she hears a female voice answer.

"Hello, Carla, it's Tanya ..."

Tanya Hot Stuff? Why is she answering his phone?

As if reading her mind, Tanya says: "Kent left his phone with me when the police took him in for questioning."

"Took him in? What are you talking about?!" Carla shouts.

Peeved by Carla's tone of voice, Tanya says: "Better speak with Ron Edwards, his lawyer, he is handling it."

"Handling what?!" screeches Carla, but the line has gone dead.

Bitch! she thinks before dialling the lawyer's number. "Mr Edwards, please, this is Carla Fowler," she says when a secretary answers the phone.

"Good day, Mrs Fowler, we have been expecting your call. Have you received the divorce papers?"

"Yes, I have, but that's not why I am calling. Where is my husband? I mean ... where is Kent?"

"Mrs Fowler, Mr Edwards is with him right now, that's all I can tell you."

Frustrated, Carla cuts the call.

Chapter Fifteen

Kent & Graham

"Tanya, I am out on bail," says Kent, straightening up in the front passenger seat of Ron Edwards' Mercedes, "but before I come home, I need to see the old folks. I think Mum and Dad went into shock when the police took him in for questioning. What did my mother say when you phoned her?"

"She did not say a word, just disconnected," answers Tanya. "Are you alright?" she adds, deep concern in her voice.

"I'll be alright once I have spoken to the oldies. I think Dad needs convincing that I had nothing to do with it all."

"I know Kent, take care – see you later."

Kent hands the borrowed phone back to the lawyer.

When they pull up in front of the Fowler's home, Kent suggests to the lawyer that he comes in with him.

"No need for a lawyer in a friendly family discussion, is there?" Ron begs off. "I will pick you up in Northcliff at 9 a.m. for our meeting with Moerane. Good night."

Kent lets himself into the house with his keys and goes through to the kitchen, where his mother gives him a sharp look.

"Didn't your father give strict instructions to keep to the law?" she demands. "Now look at you ..."

"Mum," Kent interrupts her, "I did nothing! Bobby acted on his own."

His father hastily intervenes. "Kent," he says quietly. "I have been meaning to ask you; what was that all about at the meeting: "Bang, bang ..." and cocking a finger at you?"

Kent laughs: "It's an old joke between us. Whenever you and I disagreed in a meeting, and you overruled me, Bobby would come to me afterwards, cock a finger and sing: "Bang, bang, he shot you down." Just to calm me down and make me understand who the boss is in Fowler's."

"I bloody well hope you are right. It looked to me like he was going to take the law into his own hands," says his father.

Kent looks at him pensively, before saying: "Could well be, Dad."

"I hope you understand, you have to lay charges against Bobby, otherwise you and the liquor licence go down the drain, the end of Fowlers Liquor Emporium, and all you and I have worked for."

Dorothy's deep sobs cause them both to look around at her stricken face.

"All was going so well," she wails, "until you started that *Freak club* and hired that *Hot Trash* – that's when all went wrong. Carla put all her money into that house, and then you ... you ..." she splutters, before breaking into another round of loud sobs.

"Mum," says Kent trying his utmost not to shout at his own mother, "the club is L'Afrique and Tanya's DJ name is 'Hot Stuff', as mine is 'DJ Rooster'. Carla put in the money from the sale of her salon and our house into her house in the Cape ..."

Before he can carry on, his father gets in between them. "ENOUGH!" he shouts. "Stop it! Let us find solutions instead of slinging accusations at each other."

Kent bites back his anger and says: "I have to go back to Captain Moerane tomorrow. He is evaluating all the statements tonight, and wants my decision: lay charges against Bobby, or be charged as an accomplice. I am going to try and see Bobby before I see Moerane. Sorry, but you have to take my word for it: I knew nothing about it. May I use one of your cars to go home?"

"Use your mother's car. Good night, son," says his father. When they hear her BMW reverse out and the garage door closing, his father sits down next to Dorothy on the settee in the living room. Taking her hands into his, he says: "Dotty, I think it's time for us to go back to the Old Country, don't you think?"

"Yes, ever since my sister Madge passed away last year, I have been thinking about it more and more. Her house is on the market; no one else in the family wants it. Too big and too old ..."

"Yes," Graham agrees. "We could pay the others out, restore and modernise the house, and settle in. Sutton Coldfield is a lovely area, and not far from Birmingham. I will phone your brother Harry in the morning."

"Harry, old boy, how are you doing?" asks Graham on the following day.

"Not bad, not bad, Graham," Harry replies, "apart from the gout and other old-age aches and pains."

"Tell me, Harry," says Graham, "is Madge's house still on the market?"

"Yes, it is," confirms his brother-in-law, "it's a listed building, old Tudor; no one wants to touch it, with all the planning restrictions on listed buildings; the people with money buy unlisted properties, knock the old house down and put up a new modern house. Pity really, spoils the area. By the way, Graham, why are you asking?"

As Graham reveals the recent events, Harry remarks: "Sounds like it's time, old boy. We'll take the house off the market: it's yours and Dotty's, don't you worry, we'll work something out. Come stay with me while you fix up Madge's place. I could do with some company in the pub. The familiar faces are dying out, excuse the pun," Harry cackles. "Give my love to our Dotty, will you? Call me back in a day or two. I'll bring you up to date what the rest of the family have to say."

Dorothy, who has been listening to the conversation on the speaker phone, breathes out and says: "Do you feel up to weaving a new nest, Graham?"

"Sure, why not? It will be nice to have a pint of bitter with Harry on the right side of the counter for a change."

Chapter Sixteen

Kent

Kent squeezes his mother's old 320i BMW into the undercover parking behind Tanya's Mini Cooper. Feeling somewhat weary, he decides to wait for the elevator to take him up to their penthouse apartment.

"Hello," says Tanya, leaning into him, "you look like shit. Go and strip off and I will add more hot water to the tub. What can I get you to drink?"

"What a day! Can I have an almond latte?" Tossing his clothes into the wash basket, he slips below the bubbles in the hot tub and washes the grime of the long day from his face. Coming up for air, he sees Tanya set a tray of lattes onto a side table, before dropping her sarong to join him in the spacious tub.

Sipping his almond latte, Kent relates the events from the police headquarters and later visit to his parents, omitting his mother's caustic accusations.

"What's next?" asks Tanya, removing his empty latte glass.

"Ron is picking me up in the morning to take me back for another session with Captain Moerane. He wants me to lay charges against Bobby, or admit to a conspiracy with Bobby. In the second option, Moerane will fry my ass, revoke our liquor licence, and effectively close us down."

"And if you lay charges against Bobby?" she asks.

"Bobby fries! Goes to jail for I don't know how long. Under normal circumstances it would have been a case of theft. But now, with the pandemic and the President's decree of a total lockdown and liquor sales prohibition, I don't even want to hazard a guess as to where this will go."

Tanya sinks lower into the slowly shrinking suds and says: "You have known Bobby for how many years? You trusted him implicitly. What drove him to do this now?"

Kent simply shrugs and rises to grab a bath towel for each of them. "I will try to see him before my interview with Moerane," he says. "I need to hear it from him. Plus: there is the issue of the fire in his wife's Shebeen. He most likely knows nothing of it yet, unless the police have told him to break him down."

"Oh, Kent," says Tanya, tears welling up in her eyes, "this is all so awful. Tell me, what can I do to help?"

"Nothing my love, nothing. I will sort it out in the morning and then we might change our life, yes?"

"Yes, please, Kent," Tanya replies softly, clutching his hand to her face.

Instead of Ron's Mercedes, the white Range Rover of his law firm partner, Kallie Swart, is waiting for Kent in the quiet tree-lined street of the apartment building.

"Morning," he says, as Kent gets into the passenger seat next to him, "hope you don't mind the switch, but Ron is of the opinion I am the better man for the job."

"*Goeie môre,*" Kent greets the lawyer in Afrikaans, then switches to English to add glumly: "I suppose you are right: this is not a corporate, but a criminal case."

"Afraid so," says the burly lawyer, who – despite his tailored dark suit looks more like a rural farmer about to attend the local Sunday church service. Kent knows, however, that the middle-aged, unkempt looks are deceiving. Kallie is one of the city's best criminal lawyers. "I don't suppose you've thought about much else than what lies ahead this morning," Kallie says, keeping his eyes on the increasing traffic around them. "What have you decided?"

"Kallie," says Kent, "I must see Bobby before I see Moerane. I need to hear from Bobby himself what made him do such a stupid thing."

"I'll see what I can do," says Kallie. "I take it that you want me to represent him?"

"Yes, of course; you must represent any Fowler employee involved."

"To speed things up, we should get the captain's consent for you to see Bobby. If Moerane denies you the privilege, I can see Bobby instead. He is entitled to a lawyer," says Kallie as they pull into the parking lot next to the police headquarters.

Captain Moerane gets out from behind his desk when Kent and his lawyer are shown into his office fifteen minutes later. "Mr

Swart," he says, "long time, no see. Are you going to look out for Mr Fowler?"

"Yes, sir, my corporate partner has been looking after the Fowlers forever. Never any need for my criminal expertise, but hopefully I won't be needed this time neither."

Totally ignoring Kent, Moerane replies: "The Fowlers won't need you, but one of their managers will. We have a full confession from Robert Ncobo: he states categorically that he acted against Graham Fowler's strict orders. He admitted to selling liquor to middlemen that supply shebeens in the southern suburbs. He claims that he did not steal but sold liquor during unauthorised hours. Hence there is no need for the Fowlers to lay charges: the onus is on the State. The middlemen that were caught with the liquor during the shootout with the police are in jail and will be charged by the State. As they are not Fowler employees, they are not your problem."

He stops and looks at Kent for the first time. "Goodbye, Mr Fowler, sorry for the inconvenience." Turning back to Kallie Swart he continues: "A simple case really: the state will charge Ncobo for illegal selling of liquor; a court date will be set, and you can apply for bail. The rest is up to the judicial system, which is, as you know, stretched to its limit with the pandemic and consequent increase in crime."

"Thank you, Captain Moerane," says Kallie. "When is the court hearing?"

"Ask downstairs in the charge office: they will tell you and grant you permission to see your client. If you will excuse me, I have several cases waiting."

Back in the long corridor, Swart turns to Kent: "No need for you to see Bobby: I'll bail him out first and then you can talk."

"I'll take a cab to your office ..." Kent replies.

"Just give me five minutes," Kallie cuts in, "we can go together."

Spread along the ground-floor corridors to the charge office are long queues of people, waiting to be dealt with. As Kallie pushes his way through, muttering excuses to those waiting in line, Kent is stopped by a familiar voice calling his name: "Boss, over here."

"Dumi, what are you doing here?" asks Kent.

"I was hoping to get to see Bobby," says his assistant manager.

Kent pulls him into the forecourt and tells him what transpired in Moerane's office.

"Thank God for that," says Dumi, "I don't know if you heard but Bobby's wife is okay. She and her staff ran out the back door the moment the shooting between the cops and the delivery men started. The building burnt down, but the casualties were outside: one cop and two of the delivery men."

Kent breezes a huge sigh of relief: *Thank goodness for that!*

Chapter Seventeen

Carla

"Can you frigging-well believe these people?" Carla rants, throwing her phone onto the coffee table in front of them.

Having listened to only one side of the story, Leonora pleads with her friend: "Easy, Carla, calm down. What is it?" "Don't you start patronising me. Kent is locked up and no one wants to tell me, his wife, a thing."

"Soon to be ex-wife," says Leonora, pointing at the documents on the settee next to Carla.

"How is he going to pay me alimony from jail?" she wails.

"Why don't you phone your in-laws: they will know what's going on," suggests Leonora, peeved at the way her best friend speaks to her.

Only on the following afternoon does Carla finally get to speak to Kent in Ron Edward's office. "What's going on?" she demands. "Do I have leprosy that no one wants to talk to me?"

"Sorry," says Kent, "lots of things are happening right now. Got to run ..."

"No, Kent, don't you dare hang up on me. I just wanted to tell you that I accept your settlement and won't contest it. You can tell Ron to go ahead on behalf of the both of us. I'll sign the papers and courier them up to him."

"Thanks, Carla, I'll tell him. Bye," she hears Kent say before the line goes dead. *Blast it!*

Later that evening, after Leonora has prepared one of her special lentil curries for them, the girls sit on the settee with Lex stretched out beside them and watch a re-run of "Love Affair" with Warren Beatty and Annette Benning. Halfway through the movie, Carla throws her arms around Leonora and sobs, tears streaming down her cheeks.

"Oh, Leonora, I can't believe it's over. Thirty-two years – over, finished, gone." And she bursts into a new flood of tears.

Leonora holds her close, rocking her gently in her arms, as if she were a little girl waking from a bad dream. "You are okay," she croons, stroking Carla's hair. "You are okay."

Carla's tear streaked face rises to hers, quivering lips seeking hers – seeking comfort, seeking …

The sun streaming through the open sliding doors wakes them at the same time. Disorientated, they stretch to realise that they are naked in Carla's king-size bed.

Somewhat embarrassed, Carla slides out of bed, dragging the top sheet with her as she tries to cover her body.

"Green tea?" asks Leonora, seemingly oblivious of being nude as she gets up and heads for the stairs to the downstairs open-plan kitchen. Their clothes are littered on the floor in front of the settee, with Lex stretched out on top.

"Comfortable Lex?" she asks, fishing out her rumpled, over-sized T-shirt from the day before. Slipping it over her head, Leonora switches on the kettle and prepares two mugs with green-tea bags.

Steaming mugs in hand, she goes to the table on the pool veranda, sets down their brews, strips off the clammy shirt, and takes the few steps to the pool. *Is this how it is going to be from now on?* she thinks, swimming naked from one end to the other.

"Leonora, get out, put some clothes on, we need to talk," says Carla dressed in her gym-training outfit.

As she climbs out of the pool, Carla averts her eyes and hands her a full-length sarong to drape around her.

Let her do the talking, Leonora thinks, stretching out her long legs in front of her.

"Leonora," says Carla, an embarrassed blush spreading across her face, "last night – what I mean, last night was very sweet of you. I know you care, and feel protective over me, and I appreciate your being here for me – but – last night was an exception: don't expect more than a one-night stand. I am no authority, only having slept with two men in my life, but I prefer a male in my bed."

Quick to steer the conversation away from the previous night, Leonora says: "Two men in your entire life? You mean Kent was the first and only one until Hennie?"

By now, Carla has turned scarlet. "Yes, Kent – and you know

how that went, with both of us on our individual ego trips, and Hennie, kind, considerate Hennie."

Seeing more tears welling up in her friend's eyes Leonora has to restrain herself from rushing to Carla's side. She snorts instead, "Jeez, I have had more guys than you before Angela took over."

Carla half manages a laugh, gets up and walks away to her exercise rack next to the thick floor mat.

Oh well, thinks Leonora, *back to the drawing board. Maybe it's time to move on, but where to? Not back to mother, that's for sure.*

Any plans of leaving, however, are forestalled. A couple of days later, on an early morning walk on the beach, Lex's hind legs give way. He tries to get up but sinks back with a whimper.

"Lex what is it?" Carla cries out, "Leonora, please help me get him on his feet."

"Wait, Carla, give me your car keys and I'll get the blanket. We'll carry him to the car and take him to the vet."

Close to hysterical, Carla races through the small-town traffic to the vet's clinic. Two assistants, closely followed by Carla, take Lex on a gurney into the surgery.

"Mrs Fowler," says Dr Reitz, straightening up after examining Lex carefully. "I am afraid there is little we can do for him now. The vitamin pills I prescribed previously, nor any other medication, will help him. Let him leave you with his last bit of dignity intact ..." the doctor trails off.

Carla nods; it's not her first time. "Can I hold his head in my lap?" she says bravely.

"Of course."

A couple of days later, Carla tells her gardener to dig a hole close to a newly planted King Protea shrub, large enough for the small box of Lex's ashes.

I can't leave her now, Leonora thinks with a certain amount of relief.

"I don't think I will get another dog; not for a while anyway," Carla tells her friend a few days later. "I couldn't stand leaving Lex behind by himself every time we went out. Come, Leonora, let's paint this town red."

Chapter Eighteen

Kent

Ron Edwards listens intently to Kent and Kallie's report of the morning's events at the police headquarters. "I'll get him out on bail and that's that," says Kallie. "Given the current turmoil, the case will never get to court. In time to come, we can make an application to reduce or waive the bail or get the State to accept it as an admission of guilt, with the bail amount converted to a fine."

Then he gets out of the visitor's chair in front of Ron's desk. "Keep your nose clean," he says, giving Kent a tap on the shoulder on his way out to return to his own office.

"Where were we before this mess erupted," says Ron.

"My divorce?" asks Kent.

"Right," replies the lawyer. "Carla has accepted your offer but kicked up a bit of a stink when she heard you were being investigated. Obviously concerned you would default on your alimony payments right off. Women!" He chuckles. "I will get us a date in the Magistrate's Court and let you know; fifteen minutes max and you'll be a free man."

Kent nods. "I want to have a talk with my father," he says. "I know it's a bad time, but we should sell up. The old man's been talking about returning to the UK and I desperately need a change. I can't believe I have been locked into this business for over forty years. Where has the time gone? Where has all this hard graft got me? If it weren't for the music, I would have gone crackers."

"Yes, Kent, I know what you mean. We are all caught up in our egos until it is too late."

A couple of days later, Kallie Swart phones Kent. "As I said, 25k bail with weekly reports to the closest police station to his rural farm or *kraal*. I told him to lie low, get back into his goatskin, surround himself with bare-breasted maidens, and nobody will take the slightest notice of him. I told the bailiff that you are good for the money. Is that okay with you or do you want it on the company's account?"

"No, it's right, I'll pay. Where is he now?"

"On his way to his parole district in KwaZulu-Natal or whatever they are calling it nowadays."

"Did he mention his wife at all?" Kent asks.

"Which one?" retorts Swart. "The local shebeen queen? Yes," says Kallie a little more seriously. "He phoned the moment they gave him his phone back. She is in his kraal in KwaZulu with his daughters."

"Thanks Kallie, that was a close call. Bye. Hopefully, we won't need a criminal lawyer ever again."

"Mum, Dad," says Kent to his parents after asking his father to switch his call to speaker phone. "How about dinner tomorrow night at our place? We have lots to talk about."

"*Our place?*" asks his mother, not even trying to hide her sarcasm. "You mean, YOUR place that you are sharing with that bimbo."

"Mum, please: don't go there. She is not a bimbo and, yes, we are cohabitating."

"Yes, we will come," says his father. "What time?"

"How about six p.m., the club is closed again because of the second wave of the virus."

"I know, it goes on and on. See you tomorrow," says Graham. Kent can just make out his mother's shrill voice in the background before the phone goes dead.

"Don't expect chocolates or a bunch of flowers," he says to Tanya, pulling her onto his lap.

Nuzzling into his neck, she murmurs: "Are you going to cook?"

"No, we order in a pizza or Chinese."

"Kent, be serious, you can't do that!"

"Watch this space," he says, pulling her closer.

When the ring of the intercom announces their visitors' arrival, Tanya quickly scans her image in the hall mirror. The full-length, emerald-green dress is the perfect contrast to her Titian-red hair, tied into a loose ponytail that cascades over one bare shoulder.

With a light brushing of rouge and a hint of black eyeliner, she could have stepped out of the cover of *Vogue* magazine. Satisfied, she opens the front door as the elevator door slides open.

As Graham nudges her forward, Dorothy Fowler looks uncertainly at Tanya. Stretching his hand out in greeting, Graham says: "I say, quite a change from your stage attire."

Tanya laughs, takes his right hand in her left, while proffering her right hand to Dorothy. "Hello, Dorothy," Tanya beams. "We have not met but do come in and make yourself at home."

"Hiya Mum, Dad," says Kent equally cheerfully as he comes over from the kitchen, carrying a pitcher of iced green tea. "Good to see you both."

"What a marvellous view," says Graham, looking from one side of the floor-to-ceiling sliding doors to the east and then to the other doors facing west. "When did you have the time to find this?" he asks his son.

"Thomas found it for us. We are renting with a first option to buy. Best I can do in these uncertain times."

While this exchange is taking place, Tanya has already taken Dorothy by the hand saying: "Come, let me show you the rest of this place. Apart from this open-plan living area, there are two en-suite master bedrooms, one of which we have converted into a state-of-the-art mixing studio from where we work during lockdown."

Dorothy, no longer holding back, blurts out: "You don't sound like a Russian; where did you learn English?"

Tanya produces her melodic laugh as she gently corrects the older woman: "Dorothy, I am not Russian; I am British, like you. My parents fled the Ukraine when the USSR broke up and I grew up near Oxford."

"Well, I never," says Dorothy, trying to hide her embarrassment. But, unable to let it rest she ploughs right on. "Don't you think you are a touch young for Kent?"

Tanya looks at her wide-eyed. "Funny you should say that; I have often wondered how old your son really is. With his close-cropped hair, it's near impossible to tell if he is in his twenties or forties."

"He is in his sixties," Dorothy insists.

"You don't say?" says Tanya in mock protest. On stage he carries on like a fowl ..." Breaking into a giggle, she says: "Sorry, Mrs Fowler, eh ... Dorothy, I meant rooster." She giggles again and, grabbing the older woman by the arm, she leans forward conspiratorially. "Be honest, Dorothy, given half a chance, wouldn't you have it off with Mick Jagger? And he is seventy-eight!"

No longer able to contain her own sense of humour, Dorothy blushes, giggles, and says: "I guess I would."

"You would what, Mum?" says Kent, entering the studio.

"Bonk Mick Jagger," laughs Tanya, pulling Dorothy onto the west veranda to watch the last rays of the sun setting behind the far-off mountains.

Pushing back his clean plate, Graham says: "Roast beef, veg and gravy in a plate-size Yorkshire pudding. How on earth did you manage that without a sweat, talking to Dot about bonking Mick Jagger?"

"I worked as a waitress in Windermere in the Lakes District years ago. The restaurant's speciality was a plate-sized Yorkshire pudding."

"Yes. But serving them and making them is entirely a different story," says Dorothy.

"Oh, of course, I cheated: the Yorkies are oven-ready frozen, the roast beef and gravy comes from the Deli in the village, and the veggies are from his hot-lunch counter."

"And you were against a pizza delivery or Chinese takeaway?" mocks Kent.

"Given half a chance ..." Dorothy starts.

"We know, Mum, you would bonk Mick Jagger," Kent chirps.

With the dishes packed into the washer, the four sit in the lounge, sipping coffees. "We have spoken with our Harry," says Graham, "and have come to an agreement to pay the others out for their share of the value of Madge's house. It needs some renovating, which I don't mind supervising while living with Harry for a few months," says Graham.

"That's great, Mum and Dad," says Kent, "and when will that take place?"

"As soon as the quarantines have been lifted, we will get the removers to pack up everything and ship it across to the UK to keep in storage."

"Whereabouts is the house?" asks Tanya, totally at ease in Kent's parents' company since their dinner banter.

"Sutton Coldfield in the Midlands, near Birmingham. Madge is my late sister and Harry is my older brother," says Dorothy.

"And the house here?" asks Kent.

"I don't suppose you'll want it," his father replies, "so Thomas can sell it and send us the money," says Graham. "What about you?" he continues. "What are your plans?"

"To be honest, Dad, I have lost my enthusiasm for the liquor business. If I can find a buyer, I will sell."

"And then?" asks his mother, looking at Tanya as well as her son.

"We are doing well with re-mixes. We can do that from anywhere we want – as long as we have a fast Wi-Fi connection," says Tanya, looking at Kent, who nods in agreement.

"Maybe do a world-tour as guest DJs, do Burning Man, or something like that," he adds. "Let us see how things pan out here first, if you are happy with that, Dad."

"Sure, son: go for it!"

On their way home, Dorothy says to Graham: "I don't know about you, but I have changed my mind about Tanya. She seems to be a warm and caring person, a quality I could not have accredited Carla with. She was always 'go-go-go'; more, more, more."

"Weren't they both like that?" her husband answers. "Don't you think that's the root of their drifting apart? I also worked hard but came home every night in time for dinner. Kent never did. And to be honest, I don't know how Carla put up with it for so long. You wouldn't have, would you?"

"No way," agrees Dorothy.

Meanwhile, seated on the east-facing veranda, watching the city lights blinking in the clear night sky, Kent says to Tanya: "You sure know how to win people over. I couldn't believe how you handled Mum, of all people. She was dead against you. Next moment you got her eating out of your hand."

On the following morning, Kent phones Ron Edwards just after nine a.m.

"Ron? Kent. Good morning. Put the gossip out: Fowlers Liquor Emporium is up for sale."

"Does that include Club L'Afrique?" Ron asks.

"Yes," replies Kent, "lock, stock and barrel."

"Aptly put," laughs the lawyer. "This may take a little time."

Chapter Twenty

Kent

True to his word, it had taken Graham Fowler less than a month to bring his affairs into order; get the removers in; and hand the keys of the house to Kent, to pass to Thomas, their property manager, to sell the house *voetstoots,* or 'as it is'.

Oliver Tambo International Airport is unusually quiet as Kent, Tanya, Graham and Dorothy make their way to the KLM departure counter. Dorothy is fighting back tears as reality hits her: *This is not just a holiday trip, but a permanent return to my home country.*

Graham confirms her thoughts, by saying: "This does feel strange."

Kent, who has been pushing his parents' luggage trolley turns to Tanya. "Have you considered going back to the UK?" he asks.

"Not really," she says. "It's the weather more than anything else that puts me off."

"What about your family?" asks Dot.

"They can come here on holiday when things return to normal and decide where they want to live."

"Bye," Dorothy sniffles. Embracing Tanya, she murmurs: "Take care of my son!"

A last wave and the Fowlers are ushered through to the security checkpoint area.

"What's next on the menu, Rooster?" Tanya asks playfully on their drive back to Northcliff in Johannesburg.

"Dismantle the Emporium and take a long break," he replies.

"Were you serious about 'Burning Man' the other day?" "One day, perhaps, but not right now. I fancy wallowing
in some lukewarm water, walking on unspoilt beaches, and just relaxing without a care in the world."

"Does such a place exist around here?" Tanya asks. "Oh yes," Kent replies. "We will find it," replies Kent.

But – and there is always a "but" – the changing levels of the pandemic and legislation regulating the on- and off-sales keep Kent busier than ever.

With "Hot Stuff" back in Club L'Afrique, their time together consist of a couple of sets behind the mixing tables or exhausted sleep in the early-morning hours after closing.

Although Dumisani is trying his hardest, without Bobby at his side the long hours of the job soon break his reserves.

"Ron," says Kent to his lawyer, "any nibbles yet for acquiring the business?"

"The enquiries I get are for single outlets rather than the whole lot," says Ron.

"Should we break it down?" asks Kent.

"Don't do that," advises Ron, "the plums get sold and you are left with the prunes. Just hang in there: things are picking up."

Finally, it is Thomas Banks, the group's property manager, who phones Kent.

"Good day Kent, I have a definite, confirmed buyer for your parent's house."

"That is good news," says Kent, when Thomas interrupts him.

"And – wait for it – someone that claims to know you well would like to meet with you."

"Thomas," Kent groans, "Many people claim to know me well, if they have been to the club more than twice."

"He calls himself Mister Moerane ..."

"Mister Moerane? Not Captain Moerane?" asks Kent.

"No idea. He told me 'Mister Moerane', and asked if two p.m, in his office is possible."

"His office where? Police headquarters?" Kent asks.

"No, it's in Sandton, not far from here," Thomas replies.

"Tell him 'yes' and I'll pick you up at a quarter-to. See if you can dig up some background, will you? See you later."

"I could not find a thing on Moerane, other than the captain," says Thomas as he settles down in the front passenger seat next to Kent. "All Moerane gave me was his name and a third-floor address in Sandton Mews."

It turns out that the entire third floor of Sandton Mews is

rented by Dromedaries Holdings, Liquor Import and Export. Now the penny drops for both men as they enter the reception area.

"Good day," says Thomas to the smiling receptionist, "Thomas Banks and Kent Fowler to see Mister Moerane."

"This way, gentlemen," says the receptionist, walking ahead of them toward an open office door. "Mister Moerane," she says to the man inside, "your two-thirty appointment." Then she stands aside to let them pass, closing the door behind them.

Kent just catches a glimpse of a brass plate mounted to the closing door: "SAMSON MOERANE", but no further title. When he sees this latter-day Samson, Kent has to bite his tongue to stop himself from laughing. Dressed in black pants, white shirt, and Paisley tie, Moerane does not measure more than 1,5 metres tall, if that.

Sensing Kent's amusement, a reaction to which he is obviously accustomed, Moerane cackles. "It's my nickname. We had a 'Tiny' in the class already, so my classmates named me 'Samson'." He directs them to a small conference table and gets straight to the point. "Up to now Dromedaries has focused on the import and export of liquor, mainly to our northern neighbours, as well as Madagascar, Seychelles, Mauritius, Réunion. We are now ready to expand into on- and off-sales within our own borders." He leans forward and, without asking, pours iced water into three glasses from a silver Thermos.

"My uncle, Captain Moerane," Samson continued, "told me about the spot of trouble you recently found yourself in. He got the impression you'd just about had it with the liquor business. Rumours have it that your father has retired and that you wish to sell the business. By the way," Moerane cackles," I have been to L'Afrique a couple of times; had to show my ID to prove I am over eighteen. Saw you and that Lady DJ move the crowds. You two are too hot to handle." Another loud cackle follows this endorsement.

"Now I am no bean counter, and neither are you. Why don't we shake on our intent to buy and sell, and let the accountants come up with the right numbers. What do you think of that?"

Kent likes the other man's style: let the experts come up with the numbers for the two of them to agree on. "You know that we own all the properties in which our stores are located?" he asks.

"Yes, we do, and we want them, too. How does one month sound to you to prepare the final figure?"

"Our books are up-to-date and our property portfolio is updated by Thomas Banks constantly ..."

Moerane breaks in. "We know all that. Let your and our accountants start putting actual numbers together, give some thought to an amount for goodwill, and then we can meet again in four weeks' time."

They rise and shake, while Thomas looks on without having spoken a single word.

"I like the guy," says Kent on their way back to the property manager's office.

"I agree, no BS; clear mandate: come up with the figures, then we talk."

Kent leans closer into Tanya for a better view as the Boeing 737 banks sharply for its approach to Malé's International Airport in the Maldives. Clutching his hand, she briefly turns toward him with her radiant smile. "Look at all these tiny islands floating in the crystal waters below us," she whispers in his ear.

Kent gives her hand a squeeze and smiles at her excitement. He must admit that the last five weeks have plunged him into a turmoil of emotions. The sale of Fowler's Liquor Emporium had proceeded relatively smoothly; the upsetting part had been the reaction of his long-serving management. *How could he do this? Sell them out, after years of loyal devotion to the Fowlers?* Rumours had it that some even blamed Tanya for his decision to sell. *First she busts up his marriage, and then makes him sell the business.*

How could he convince them otherwise? Were they right? Quite honestly, he did not know himself; all he realises now is that his marriage to Carla had been quite conventional. They had each followed their own careers, like most couples do. Because they had been highly ambitious, they had driven themselves harder than others might have done to achieve their individual goals, but never a common goal. Having had no children, their house had never been a home: merely a place to own, to sleep, and to contain one's possessions. Even sleeping in had become sporadic when he had started Club L'Afrique.

He had to admit that it had been Tanya who had convinced him that two people could share one passion, one goal, and that the shared passion might grow into a love for each other.

The bump of the wheels hitting the runway brings him back to the present: the longed-for holiday!

After clearing immigration and customs, they are alerted by an announcement over the Tannoy: "Messieurs van der Walt, Hart, and Fowler to Information please." Followed by the same announcement a second later.

A white-robed local greets them at the counter: "Welcome to the Maldives. Please follow me to your transfer to the Malé South Atoll."

The humidity hits them before the heat, as they cross to the waiting minibus that will take them to the nearby port. The cabin of the luxurious high-speed ferry is air-conditioned, and their local guide is quick to hand out chilled and scented towels and frosted glasses of a tropical fruit juice concoction as "welcome drinks". As the captain navigates the boat slowly through the busy port's entrance, the guide announces that their transfer will take less than twenty minutes.

Somewhat disappointed, Tanya says: "I thought we would be further out from Malé."

No sooner has she spoken, when the captain opens the throttles of the twin engines, and the ferry virtually lifts out of the water to fly past all the other boats. They pass atoll after atoll with varying styles of bungalows perched on stilts above tranquil, shallow waters, or palm-shaded A-frames set on white-sand beaches, bordered by coral reefs and the turquoise Indian Ocean.

Tying up at a wooden jetty that extends over the edge of the coral reef, their guide takes them for a walk to the reception building. The demarcated, path of equally white sand is meticulously raked, while the gardeners are busy sweeping up fallen leaves on either side of them. "Mosquito and Sand-fly control," explains their guide, "by continuous raking they have nowhere to breed, otherwise you would not be able to sleep or enjoy your stay."

A large map of the island, reminiscent of an upside-down

teardrop, is displayed on the wall behind the reception desk. Luigi, the resort manager of Italian origin, explains: "On the wider top of the island we are protected from the current by a protruding reef formation. Not only does it protect the island, but it also divides the current to flow down both sides at an equal rate. This reef submerges from half a metre to a depth of three metres along both sides of the island protecting the beaches. Here, right at the bottom, the thinnest part of the island, the beach feathers out to a thin sandbank, where the currents reunite.

"Walking on top of the reef is forbidden. One must walk on the boardwalks across the reef and climb down three steps to get into the water. We recommend that you enter the water via this boardwalk closest to the restaurant's sundeck, and let the current take you all the way to the sandbank. The sun illuminates the left reef in the mornings, and the righthand reef in the afternoon. Next to the map you can see some photographs and the names of the fish you will encounter."

The receptionist then issues Kent the keys to their A-framed bungalow. "It is the furthest and most secluded bungalow right next to this long sandbank. You can walk there on the beach or on the central walkway in the shade of the trees. Our porters have deposited your luggage on your veranda already. Please enjoy your stay."

"Let's walk in the shade for now," says Tanya, slinging her light backpack over one shoulder. "There'll be plenty of time for sun-tanning once we have changed and settled."

The A-frame nestles in a small clearing of palm trees, overlooking a shallow bay formed by the white sandbank, which stretches out into the turquoise waters like a curved tongue. Having only glass at the front, the A-frame has a comfortable, spacious lounge with a mezzanine floor suspended above for the king-size bed. A group of sun-loungers on the veranda and the beach further on beckon them outdoors.

Not wasting a moment, Kent strips off, slips on swimming trunks, and takes the ten or twelve steps needed to throw himself into the warm, shallow ocean, followed less than a minute later by a bikini-clad Tanya.

"Is that what you had in mind when you fantasised about

wallowing in warm water?" she asks, sliding on top of him and pushing his head under water. Then they end up tumbling,while shrieking and choking for air.

After breakfast on the following morning, the couple take Luigi's advice and walk to the top of the island, crossing the reef on the boardwalk, and taking to the water less than a metre away from the face of the reef. Not bothering with flippers, they pull their goggles over their eyes, clean the snorkel with a sharp blast of breath, and observe the underwater world which they pass as they are gently pushed by the current. Over half an hour later, they have drifted past the length of the island, and lie like beached seals back on the sandbank in front of their A-frame.

"That has to be one of the most amazing underwater scenes I have ever experienced!" Kent exclaims.

"Surreal, and we did not have to do a thing: the current just slid us past the entire reef. Did you feel the angel fish nibbling at you? Thank goodness they weren't sharks," says Tanya.

Having eaten lunch, they drift down the leeward side of the island with the reef illuminated by the afternoon sun. Kent and Tanya agree that they saw less fish, and that there had been a swell trying to push them against the reef, forcing them to stay further away.

Even later in the shower together, they notice the sun's effect on their pale bodies. "It will be T-shirts in and out of the water tomorrow," they grin in unison.

After a delicious dinner of grilled fish and salads, they take their coffees outside to enjoy on the deck.

"Hot Stuff! Is that you?!" shouts a tall man, jumping up from his deckchair close by.

"Mumbo Jumbo? I don't believe it!" replies Tanya excitedly, jumping up as well to embrace the other man. She drags him across to where Kent is now also out of his deckchair.

"Hey, I am DJ Rooster, pleased to meet the legendary DJ Mumbo Jumbo at last," says Kent.

"What is this shit? A fucking DJ convention in the Maldives?" asks Mumbo, crooking a finger at a young raven-haired girl to join them. "Cherry, baby, meet DJs Hot Stuff and Rooster in person."

"Hi, you two," replies Cherry sinking into one of the additional deckchairs a waiter has pulled up for them. With everyone all talking at the same time, the conversation is not going anywhere.

"Hold it guys," Tanya laughs. "One couple at a time, please. Mumbo, you start: what are you doing here?"

"Well, if you insist. I just finished a three-month gig at White's sky bar in Dubai. Cherry and I hooked up about a month ago and decided to go for a swim in this part of the world before my next gig in LA. Now you Hot Stuff, what's up with you?"

"Well, if you insist," she mimics Mumbo to everyone's hoots of laughter. "I just finished a lengthy gig in South Africa, hooked up with Rooster, and decided to come for a swim in this part of the world before my next gig in ... Where is our next gig, Rooster?" More merriment greets that last remark.

"To be honest," says Kent, "I haven't had a chance to think about it, with my Club L'Afrique subjected to constant changes in lockdown regulations. Now that the sale is concluded, we are open to suggestions."

Tanya adds: "While Rooster was busy with the sale, I carried on with international re-mixes."

"Way to go," Mumbo agrees.

Without intruding on one another's privacy, the two couples still manage to meet up most nights over coffee to talk about current trends in the international music industry.

"What's it like in South Africa?" asks Cherry, whose complexion is nearing ebony from spending all day in the sun and salt water.

"It's great," says Hot Stuff, "I am loving it."

"You are biased," says Mumbo, "by 'loving it' you are referring to the Rooster, right?"

Blushing unnoticeably under her newly acquired tan, she admits: "I suppose you are right."

The remaining days of their holiday on the Malé South Atoll pass far too quickly for both couples. Promising to keep in touch, Mumbo Jumbo and Cherry leave for their journey to LA; followed a day later by Kent and Tanya, who return to South Africa.

To finalise matters, Kent spends time with his firm of accountants; his lawyer, Ron Edwards; and Thomas Banks, the property manager.

His accountants present him with an updated account of his personal affairs, which are – even after paying out his father – very satisfactory. Ron will carry on handling Kent's future business contracts, while Thomas has joined the Dromedaries group to continue managing the growing property portfolio.

"What are your plans regarding the Northcliff penthouse? Are you going to take up the option to purchase?" Thomas asks Kent over lunch.

"No, Thomas, as nice as the place is, we want to leave the city and travel around for a while, maybe visit some out-of-the-way country *dorps,* meet some folks that left the rat race years ago, and see where we fit in."

"You surprise me," says Thomas. "I thought you and Tanya would have left South Africa to cash in on the global scene."

"Thomas, this may surprise you, but Tanya thinks we can bring the global scene here. Financially, with our weak currency, it would make a lot of sense for artists to compose, write, and record in this country."

"Interesting," Thomas muses aloud, signalling the waiter for the bill.

Chapter Twenty-One

Carla

"Yes, I got it," says Carla, listening to Micky's instructions as to how to find his place, "but why are your directions to a Port Elizabeth address? I thought you lived in Uitenhage."

"I do during the week," Micky replies, "but on the weekends I live in PE. I'll explain when I see you. We finish at three o'clock on Fridays, allowing two hours for the 140-kilometre commute, I get home around five p.m. If you leave your place around two o'clock, we should be good." Before disconnecting, he confirms cheerfully: "See you then. Take it easy and watch out for speed traps."

Why are men so open-ended? Carla thinks, swapping from a hold-all to a bigger case. *Maybe meet some friends, maybe go kayaking ... don't men know that a woman requires completely different wardrobes for these two activities alone, never mind times in between, and – Jeez – what about at night? PJs or Nighty? Don't forget the dressing gown! Is kayaking better suited for a bikini or a one-piece costume?*

She finally settles on a medium-sized suitcase and a hold-all, plus a toiletry bag. *Port Elizabeth is a city, not a dorp: if I forget something, I can still go and buy it.*

Just outside Humansdorp, a traffic policeman jumps out from behind a concrete bridge column.

"Shit, shit, shit!" Carla cries out, pulling over and off the highway as required by the cop.

"Where is the fire, lady?" asks the policeman, listening intently to a message coming over the intercom. "152,5 kilometres per hour in a 100-kilometres per-hour zone. I'm afraid I will have to take you in."

Rendered completely speechless, Carla reacts by opening the waterworks. As the mascara from two hours before streaks down her cheeks, Carla finds her voice to plead. "I am so sorry, officer," she sobs, "this car of mine is far too powerful for me. I misjudged the speed I was travelling at."

The law enforcement officer nods his head in agreement. "These *blêrrie* Mercedes Estate cars should not be driven by ladies who are hardly able to look over the top of the steering wheel, hey?"

Carla is about to unleash her tongue at that remark, when she bites her cheek and says instead. "What type of car would you recommend for me, officer?" she says demurely.

"Nothing that goes faster than one twenty," says the cop with a straight face, handing her the ticket. "Five hundred rand, to be paid within thirty days at the Humansdorp Traffic Department. If you want to defend the fine, you have thirty days to do so. Failing to do either is considered contempt of court and punishable with a jail sentence."

Relieved to have gotten off so lightly, Carla stuffs the traffic fine into the side pocket of her handbag, thanks the traffic officer, and gets back onto the freeway.

"Did you get lost?" Micky asks, opening the gate to his driveway for her.

"No, I got stopped for a speeding fine," Carla replies, "and don't you dare tell me that you warned me."

"Come inside," Micky grins, pointing to the open front door of the single-storey bungalow. "We will get your things just now." Built in the 1970s or 80s, it is the only remaining, single-storey building, surrounded by more recent, double-storey homes.

A parquet-floor passage leads past closed doors to an open-plan kitchen with sliding, glass-paned doors, opening onto a piece of lawn with sweeping views of Algoa Bay beyond.

"I was born here," Micky says. "My parents bought the plot in the sixties and built this house in 1978. I came along a couple of years later, after my parents had given up all hope of children. Do you have children?" he asks her.

"No time," Carla tells him.

"No time to try or no time to have?" Micky asks, unexpectedly serious.

"Both," she says and changes the subject. "You stay here on the weekends and during the week?"

"I own a bachelor flat in the better part of Uitenhage where most management staff stay," he says. "It is only a place to shower, sleep, and have breakfast in really. I share a housekeeper with three other tenants, which works very well. When she is off, I am here. This place is looked after by Philemon, a Malawian gardener and housekeeper who has already worked for my parents before they were killed in a car accident in the Eastern Cape."

Now Micky changes the subject. "How much kayaking have you done before?"

"None, really," she admits.

"Okay, then we will start in the shallow of the lagoon, by teaching you how to right yourself if you accidentally turn over."

Just after ten, Micky helps Carla with her bags.

"I didn't realise you are moving in, otherwise I would have made some wardrobe space for you," he laughs.

"The others just bring a change of knickers and a toothbrush?" she chirps him.

He blushes but does not comment.

"You can use the bathroom next to the bedroom, I go down the passage to shower," he suggests as she is trying to organise herself.

Carla is in bed when he comes back from the shower, with the bath towel wrapped around his waist. Self-consciously switching off the remaining bedside lamp, he drops the towel on the floor and slides into bed beside her. Carla moves around nervously until Micky finally gets his arm around her to pull her closer.

"Micky," she whispers, "I am not very good at this, you are the third guy in my life."

He stops her by closing his mouth gently over hers.

The lagoon Micky takes them to the next morning, has a narrow, sandy beach with clear, shallow water extending more than fifteen metres, before dropping away. Carla helps Micky lift the twin-seater kayak from the roof rack of his Audi, and into the water. "Wear a one-piece costume, a T-shirt, and a baseball cap, if you want to avoid being burnt by the sun," Micky had told her after a quick Muesli and coffee breakfast.

Now, as they lower the kayak into the lagoon, he says: "You sit in front, me in the back; you paddle, I paddle and steer. Once we have that right I will warn you and turn us over in shallow water.

Lean to the right, dig your paddle into the sand and push. That should turn us upright. If not, you slide out of your seat, surface, and turn the kayak back to shore, as getting back in deeper water may be too difficult to start with.”

Carla surprises Micky with her upper-body strength and soon they are on their way up the river that feeds the lagoon.

The weekend passes far too quick for both of them.

“Coming back next weekend?” Mickey asks, as he kisses her goodbye on the following Monday morning in the driveway of his house.

“Yes, I would like that, toy-boy,” says Carla, pushing herself against him suggestively. Micky grins, slaps her playfully on the behind before getting into his car to leave for work.

“Watch your speed,” is the last thing she hears as she gets into the Mercedes to start her drive home.

Stopping for a coffee at the Tsitsikama Petroport, Carla pulls her phone out of her bag for the first time since leaving her house on Friday. As it boots up, she sees twelve missed calls and messages. All from Leonora; each one sounding more desperate than the previous.

Feeling awful, Carla dials Leonora’s number. “Where the fuck are you? I sent the complex security and the cops to the house twice. *No one home, no car in the garage,* is all I got.”

“Sorry, Leonora, I went to PE ...”

“You went where? What the hell are you doing in PE?” asks Leonora her voice now turning bitter.

“I spent the weekend with Micky in his house in PE, do you mind?” Carla replies defiantly.

“I don’t care who you ball but leave your phone on or at least let me know. Don’t just disappear under the radar,” says Leonora.

“Sorry, I didn’t think,” Carla replies. Wanting to gain back some ground, she quickly adds: “How are you and Brenda getting on?”

“Mind your own bloody business!” Leonora flares up again. “We are getting on just fine. In fact, the reason I phoned in the first place was to let you know that I am thinking of staying on.”

“Great,” says Carla, feeling her own heckles coming up. “Stay all you want. I am just going to be around until Friday lunchtime, then I am going back to PE for the weekend.”

Instead of a reply, however, the call is disconnected.

See if I care, Carla thinks and gathers her bag to walk to the exit.

That Monday afternoon she puts on a wash; Tuesday and Wednesday she works out in her home gym and lolls around the pool; Thursday the gardener comes, and she decides to clean the house. Before she knows it, it is Friday again and she is packing for the weekend in PE.

Is this how it is going to be from now on? she thinks as she eases the Mercedes onto the N2 East freeway, carefully setting her speed control. *Next week I must leave earlier and pay that fine in Humansdorp on my way through,* she reminds herself.

It rains virtually all weekend and Micky quite cheerfully pronounces it a *"Stay-in-bed weekend"*.

"If John Lennon and Yoko Ono could stay in bed for three days, why can't we?" he asks, pulling Carla on top of him.

"If you are up to it," she giggles.

On the following Friday morning after that, Micky phones Carla early in the morning: "Don't come all the way to PE, meet me in the central beach parking lot in J-Bay instead."

"Do you mean Jeffrey's Bay?" she asks.

"Yes, no one calls it by its proper name anymore, it's just 'J-Bay'. I booked us a room in a B&B right on the beach."

"Oh goody," she says," I hope it rains again. You are turning me into a nymphomaniac."

"A what?" he asks, but she has already disconnected to repack her bag.

Carla spots Micky's Audi as she turns into the Central Beach parking lot just after five p.m.

"Why are we meeting in J-Bay," she asks, freeing herself from his passionate welcome embrace.

"This is where I used to spend my weekends surfing," he says.

"You surf?" she asks.

"Used to, but two years ago it lost its attraction," he says with a slight shiver.

"What happened," she asks.

"We were surfing at the Point, maybe twenty of us, sitting or lying on our boards, waiting for a curl to build; when I hear a guy scream less than twenty meters away. Then a flurry of a triangular fin, a tail thrashing and the water turning red. Sharks! What could we do? We scream, paddle like shit, some to get away, some to help. Fortunately, the National Sea Rescue Institute boat was out there. They got him out and a sea-rescue helicopter rushed him off. He survived but was badly lacerated."

"How terrible! Did you know him?"

"No, we were told he was a 40-year-old, experienced surfer from Cape Town," says Micky, wiping his brow as if trying to wipe away a bad dream. "I sold my surfboard the next day and never went in again. Bought the kayak and stuck to the lagoon and rivers where sharks don't go."

On this weekend, they walk the beaches and feast on seafood in J-Bay's popular Kitchen Window restaurant. On the following Monday morning, when Carla switches her phone back on, she finds a message from Leonora:

COMING BACK MONDAY LUNCHTIME ON INTERCAPE BUS. PLEASE MEET ME AT SHELL ULTRA CITY, I'LL TEXT YOU THE ETA. L.

"What a nerve!" Carla exclaims.

Chapter Twenty-Two

Kent & Tanya

"Where would you like to live?" asks Kent, spreading out a map of South Africa in front of Tanya.

"How can I decide that from a map?" she asks, looking at the representation of a vast country comprising: coastlines, green forested areas, high mountains, and deserts. "Couldn't we tour around? Start in the north, head east from there, then south, and up the West Coast?" she asks.

Kent bursts out laughing. "Typically female," he says, "leaving all the options open."

Tanya crinkles her nose and gives Kent one of her mischievous smiles. "Isn't that why you guys love us? Because of all the options that we offer?"

"Okay then, get packing: we leave for the Mpumalanga when you are ready."

"I am ready, let's leave tomorrow morning," she replies, throwing her arms around him.

"Is that all you are taking?" Kent asks when she hands him one hold-all to stow in the boot of the Cayenne Turbo.

"Sure," she grins. "I can wash my G-strings at night and they are dry in the morning, and T-shirts and hoodies are sold in every village store. We are travelling light, getting away from it all, right?"

"Yes, you are right. I'm just not used to that simple way of thinking from a woman."

"Better get used to it," Tanya smiles, buckling up in her seat.

"Where are we headed?" she asks, as he selects the lane turning onto the freeway heading north.

"How about some game watching: lion, leopard, rhino, buffalo, and elephant?" he asks.

"All together?" she asks in all innocence. "Are you taking me to a Zoo?" Then she bursts out laughing. "Of course! The Kruger National Park!"

"Why not? You have not had much of a chance to see Africa, have you?"

Seven hours later, with a couple of stops along the way, Kent and Tanya pull up at the entrance to one of South Africa's premier private game reserves, bordering the Kruger National Park.

"Why here and not in the bigger Kruger Park?" Tanya asks.

"You may come across larger herds of one type of animal," Kent replies, "but you may also drive around for days without seeing more than a couple of zebras or impalas. In the smaller reserves, the groups are smaller and more condensed. This reserve is well known for its leopards, which you will be very lucky to see in the Kruger. Apart from that, you will enjoy the accommodation here far more."

Half an hour later, a porter places their bags on a luggage rack and pulls back the blinds of the glass doors that lead onto a suspended wooden deck.

"Please keep your windows and doors closed when you leave your bungalow," says the porter, pointing to a group of monkeys swinging and jumping among the branches of a nearby tree. "They love to see what they can steal, especially the contents of the fruit bowl."

But Tanya is already on the deck, pointing excitedly to a group of elephants at the edge of the waterhole: "Look at the baby," she exclaims. "How tiny it is next to its mother!"

Over the next hour, as the sun disappears behind the undulating hills on the horizon, a steady stream of game make their way to the wide waterhole. Kent, who has been in the Kruger Park, as well as quite a few private game ranches, simply smiles at Tanya's fascinated outbursts. *"Look there! Look at the giraffe: how wide it must spread its front legs to drink! Look at the warthog: how their tails stand up like a car's aerial when they run! Look, look, look ..."*

At around seven p.m., a Land Rover drops off a chef and a waiter who busy themselves in the courtyard kitchen adjacent to the bungalow's entrance. Not fifteen minutes later, Kent and Tanya are served a variety of appetizers; a main course of grilled venison steaks, sautéed vegetables, and salads; followed by a tropical fruit salad and ice cream.

"Wow, that was amazing!" they both agree, when the chef and the waiter wish them a pleasant evening. A Land Rover with a game ranger arrives to collect the two men. While they are busy loading their utensils and cool boxes, the ranger taps on the door and enters on Kent's invitation.

"Good evening," he greets the couple, "I am Johan Coetzee, your game ranger on tomorrow morning's game drive. Your wake-up call is at 5.30 a.m. and I will be here at 6 a.m. It's nippy in the mornings, so please wear something warm. Once the sun is up it gets warm quickly."

"What can we expect to see tomorrow?"

Picking up on her foreign accent, the ranger asks with a smile.

"First time in the bush, Madam?"

"Yes, but please stop calling me 'Madam'. I am Tanya and this is Kent."

"Thank you, Tanya and Kent. To answer your question: over the past few weeks, I have been busy compiling a series of photographs of a leopard mum and her two cubs since their birth. I am compiling a book I want to publish. We will visit them and see what else we come across along the way."

"How exciting! See you at six o'clock," says Tanya as the ranger retreats to take the chef and the waiter back to the main camp.

Several times during that night, Kent and Tanya are woken by growling and the roars of nearby lions. At 5.30 their telephone chirps with their wake-up call, and at six sharp the ranger pulls up in a game- viewing Land Cruiser with a tracker's seat mounted up front and with a raised viewing platform for the two of them.

"Morning," says Johan, "meet Rufus, our tracker. He sits up front, analysing the different spoors that we will come across as we drive to the leopard's lair."

Grateful for the blankets, Kent and Tanya sit huddled together in the cool morning breeze as they advance through low brush, open plains, and taller thorn trees. On Rufus' hand signal, Johan slows or stops for the couple to spot the sightings of antelope, zebra, a lone buffalo bull, rhino, and an elephant who blocks the road in front of them.

Johan stops to explain that they are now close to the leopard family's clearing which is dominated by an old, thickly branched tree, with an array of stumps and fallen trees around it. Approaching the clearing at very low speed, with the wind blowing in their direction, they can smell and hear the squabbling cubs before they can see them behind a rotten piece of tree trunk.

Rufus points to a fork of a thick branch some three metres off the ground where the female leopard has dragged a small bush buck to protect it from the fangs of wild dogs and hyenas. It is some of the insides of the dead buck that the cubs are squabbling over, as Johan's immense telephoto lens zooms in on the scene, to capture these images for his planned book.

Half an hour later, with the sun now filling the clearing and the wild cats stretched out safely in the lower branches of the shady tree, the Land Cruiser inches away slowly to return to the camp for breakfast.

Three exciting days later, the couple leave the private game ranch to continue through parts of Swaziland into the northern part of KwaZulu-Natal, the traditional home of the proud amaZulu warriors. On their second and last night in the Hluhluwe-Umfolozi Rhinoceros Reserve, Tanya says to Kent: "Thank you, my love, for showing me Africa's wild side. Can I be honest? I have had enough of game viewing for a while. Can we have a change of scenery?"

Quite relieved himself, Kent pulls out the map of South Africa and places it on the coffee table in front of their settee. Tracing a route with his index finger, he suggests: "Down the KZN coast to Durban; one overnight stop; then up into the Drakensberg, cut across through the Golden Gate area of the north- eastern Free State; and get onto the N1 south to Cape Town. How does that sound?"

Tanya, who has followed his finger along the way, says: "Sounds like a lot of driving to me, is that okay with you?"

"Sure, we go as far as we feel each day, find a place to spend the night, and carry on."

Ten days later, Kent and Tanya's future is decided over dinner on a small wine estate, spectacularly surrounded by the Klein Drakenstein mountains.

Chapter Twenty-Three

Carla

"You've got a nerve: you know that don't you?" Carla snarls, as Leonora opens the boot of the Merc to deposit her suitcase.

"And a wonderful day to you, too," says Leonora, getting into the front passenger seat beside her friend. The drive to Carla's home is cloaked in silence, with both women determined not to be the first to speak.

"Where have you been all this time?" Carla finally explodes after Leonora has unpacked her case and come down to the living room.

"In Cape Town with Brenda: she wants to help me to get back into event planning. She says I don't need all these partners; I should plan small intimate events, nothing over one hundred people. We spent a couple of days looking at venues I could hire. With the winelands all around there is a massive choice and it got me all motivated again. Then she introduced me to contract caterers and an agent with singers, bands, and even full orchestras. I tell you, Carla, the greater Cape Town area is so vibrant; why don't you sell this place and find something around Cape Town, then you will have the best of all worlds."

Softening up, Carla says: "I am glad for you. I never liked your partners: you brought the work in on a platter, and they took all the credit."

"True, but they did give me a chance. I knew very little about event planning: all I knew was how to wait at tables and up-sell off a menu," Leonora responds, before changing the subject. "How are things with Toyboy?"

"His name is Michael, or Micky, and he is not a toyboy. He is a very nice guy with manners. He is considerate and comes up with great ideas for our weekends together."

Leonora rolls her eyes, "How many years younger than you is he? Twenty? Twenty-five? How long will it take for a younger body to turn his head?"

"What's wrong with my body?" says Carla, "I make forty-year-olds look like grannies."

"At the moment, dearie; wait until all that muscle starts to look like Egyptian parchment."

"Get out of here, you bitch!" Clara snaps. "Go back to Cape Town to your 'girl friends'. Micky is not a sponger like you: he has never allowed me to pay for anything, ever! You have been living here forever without ever contributing a thing, especially in the beginning when I was struggling before Kent started paying alimony."

With a last poisonous look, Leonora pulls her phone out of her pocket and speed dials: "Chris? Leonora, can you come and pick me up in half an hour? ... Yes, great; can I stay the night? Great – tomorrow I am going back to Cape Town."

With that she storms up to the guest bedroom to pack her belongings.

It's only when Carla enters her bedroom hours later, after watching a movie on TV, that she sees her purse, lipstick, and hairbrush on her dressing table with a brief note:

TOOK MY HANDBAG I LENT YOU MONTHS AGO. L.

"As if I need your bloody bag," Carla growls, before heading to the shower.

Maybe Leonora is right, she thinks before going to sleep. Maybe I should sell up, not to move to Cape Town but to Port Elizabeth, to be closer to Micky.

Chapter Twenty-Four

Kent & Tanya

"You are my only guests tonight, shall we dine together?" asks Ottmar Ellerine, proprietor of the Kleine Draken Wine Estate.

"We would love to," says Kent, after a quick enquiring glance at Tanya.

"Shall we say six forty-five for a pre-dinner drink?" suggests Ottmar.

"The time is perfect," says Tanya, "can the pre- dinner drink be non-alcoholic?"

"Certainly ... for both of you?" the vineyard proprietor asks.

When Kent nods his affirmation, Ottmar asks: "But, excuse me, why did you choose to stay at a wine estate, if you don't drink alcohol?"

"You won't believe this, but my father and I owned Fowler's Liquor Emporium until a month or two ago. We came here because we loved the serene look of the place, and the excellent reviews on your website, booking.com, and TripAdvisor: all 'Superb' and 'Excellent'. We don't think those reviews were written under the influence of your Gold Label wines."

Ellerine laughs heartily at Kent's response and says: "Freshen up, I'll see what I can come up with."

At 6:20 that evening, Tanya is pirouetting in front of Kent, dressed in a frock so crinkled that it is a fashion statement instead of a disaster.

"Wow!" says Kent, "that looks stunning on you."

Tanya curtsies. "I saw it in a Melbourne boutique and knew it would come in handy one day."

Fortunately for Kent, their host is dressed in a pair of jeans and open-neck sports shirt as well. Seeing Kent's relief, he says: "I noticed that you are travelling light when you checked in. To be honest, that's how I dress the moment I am off duty." He points to a round table expertly set for three persons. A young waiter approaches, opens a bottle of white wine and, starting with

Tanya, pours three glasses.

Ellerine raises his glass. "*Zum Wohl*. Don't look so worried my dear, I have not forgotten your request, this is non-alcoholic wine, one of my experiments. When the government decided to stop the sale of alcohol, I took the alcohol out of my last harvest and kept my business alive. I invested in the spinning-cone filtration process and am achieving remarkable results, as you will be able to judge for yourself. Pardon my manners: my first name is Ottmar, may I use Tanya and Kent?"

The conversation stays with non-alcoholic wine production until their meal of Cape Malay Green Bean Bredie arrives: a fragrant stew of lamb neck, green beans, and spices, accompanied by another non-alcoholic, but robust Shiraz from Ottmar's estate.

"This is delicious," says Tanya. "The flavours complement each other exquisitely."

"Where are you from, Tanya?" Ottmar asks, once they have changed to comfortable recliners on the veranda of the beautifully restored Cape Dutch homestead. "I hear too many different accents to hazard a guess."

"Born in the Ukraine, raised in the UK, and travelled a lot in my job," says Tanya.

"Which is?" asks Ottmar.

"I am in the music business: disc jockey, re-mixer, producer, songwriter."

"My goodness," says Ottmar, "I had you down for a dancer or fashion model."

"That, too," says Tanya, giving Kent a big smile, "but music is our passion."

"Our?" asks Ottmar, quick to pick up on the nuances of her reply.

"We are both passionate about music," Kent chips in, "that's how we met: in my night club."

"Well, I never, you own a night club?"

"Used to, sold the lot," says Kent.

"And now?" insists their host inquisitively.

"Now we are looking for a special place to build a new future together," says Tanya. "What about you, though: you are not from this part of the world."

"Indeed not, I am from the Baltic seacoast in Germany. I worked in a boatyard, specialising in round-the-world sailing yachts, hand-crafted and expensive. When I came into an unexpected inheritance from an obscure family member; I built my own yacht and left Germany for good."

Quite fascinated, Kent asks: "And how did you end up here?"

"Someone stole my yacht when my crew and I went ashore in Cape Town. It was not the first attempt: it is a stunning yacht that caused a lot of envy. I was offered staggering sums wherever we moored for any length of time. That time they got away with it."

Taking a sip from a fresh cup of coffee which the young waiter had unobtrusively poured for them, Ottmar continues: "They did not get far though. A bad storm must have caught them, or they were amateurs. The yacht was spotted by some rock fishermen up the West Coast. The registration was traced by Lloyds to me, and now I have just finished restoring her, and am eager to get back on the water. I will show her to you after breakfast; the hangar is just across the road."

"What about the wine estate?" asks Kent.

"Up for sale, but who wants to buy a wine farm now, with the pandemic and all the economic uncertainties?"

They chat for a while longer before turning in for the night, after agreeing to have breakfast together at 8.30.

"Thomas? It's Kent. Sorry to disturb you so late," says Kent when his ex-property manager answers his phone. After a few moments of pleasantries, Kent gets to the point; five minutes later Thomas agrees to get back to him the next day.

Tanya, who has taken the opportunity to laze in the hot tub in their spacious en-suite bathroom, joins him just as he places the smart phone on the bedside table.

They are just busy with their order of smoked salmon omelettes and freshly baked croissants, when Kent's phone crows. Excusing himself from the table he takes a couple of steps into the garden before looking at the caller ID.

"Morning, Thomas," he says, "I did not expect to hear from you so early."

"Morning Kent, it was easy, he gave it to every agent in the telephone book. Difficult site to sell, most of the property is on the other side of a secondary road. And," says Thomas, "it consists of a rocky, wooded gorge leading up into the mountains. Useless for grapes, maybe okay for mountain goats. The part you and the manor house are on is barely breaking even and reliant on overseas tourists, which are not coming."

"Thomas," Kent replies, "do me a favour: put in a cheeky offer of fifty percent off the asking price from an undisclosed client."

"But why do you want a wine farm? You don't even drink," says Thomas.

"Just do it, please. I have a gutfeel for this place."

Returning to the table, he finds his breakfast gone, to be replaced minutes later by a fresh plate.

Half an hour later, Ottmar stops in front of a large hangar behind a heavy security gate and fencing topped with razor wire. CCTV cameras are visible all over, plus many more that are hidden they can't spot. "Not taking any more chances with her, in or out of the water," he says, tapping a code into the alarm system. The top-hung hangar doors slide back with the push of one finger, to reveal the gleaming sweep of an all-wooden hull stretching high above them.

"My goodness!" Tanya exclaims with a sharp intake of breath.

"A work of art," Kent agrees, looking around the immense hangar that must be over five metres high and more than twelve metres deep.

"Twelve by eight by five," Ottmar confirms, seeing Kent's calculative glance.

After admiring the yacht for over an hour and listening to Ottmar's in-depth explanation of the satellite GPS system, the size of the twin Sulzer in-board diesel engines, salt-water purifiers, solar cells, and sail configuration, they are left in no doubt that this man does not belong on dry land, but on the wide-open oceans.

"Can I have a look behind this hangar up the gorge?" asks Kent. "Of course," says Ottmar, "it is like a natural amphitheatre with clearings until the treeline ends and gives way to brush and eventually just the grey rock of the Klein Drakenstein mountains."

"It's beautiful," says Tanya, eyes gleaming in awe of what unfolds in front of them.

The ringtone of Ottmar's phone interrupts the quiet. "Yes?" he says, shrugging his shoulders apologetically, turning away from the couple. "... That's less than half of what I asked for by the time you take off your commission!" they hear him shout, "how serious are they? ... A cash offer? Seriously? ... Jeez, the first offer for over a year! Cut your commission in half and accept the offer. What's that phrase – *voetstoots?* ... Oh, all inclusive? ... Yes, of course, can't take anything with me on my yacht, other than a case or two of our Gold Label reserves. I will load them before they come to take stock."

Ottmar comes back to join Kent and Carla. "Sorry, you two, for the interruption," he explains, "but someone has just put in a cash offer for the estate. Only fifty percent of my asking price, but what the heck? I want to get going."

To Tanya's amazement, Kent stretches his hand out to Ottmar. "Would you care to shake on it?"

"Shake on it?" says a bewildered Ottmar, "shake on it?" As the penny drops, he says: "Well, I'll be damned! A tea-tootler buys my wine estate! What on earth for?"

Kent points at the hangar and says: "For this!"

"Oh no!" cries Ottmar. "The yacht is not part of the deal."

"I am not interested in your yacht, I mean the hangar."

Looking totally confused Ottmar says: "What do you want with the hangar?"

"I'll tell you over dinner," grins Kent, pulling the laughing Tanya close to him.

Chapter Twenty-Five

Carla

At first, Carla is relieved to have the house to herself. She cleans out what was previously referred to as "Leonora's Room" and converts it into a proper guest bedroom with all the little luxury touches she had enjoyed in the five-star accommodation Kent had treated them to occasionally, *before Club L'Afrique,* she thinks. *How seldom I think of Kent lately.*

Satisfied that the house is now exactly the way she wants it, Carla gets on with her routine. From Friday afternoon to Monday morning, she spends time with Micky. Tuesday, Wednesday, and Thursday, she spends at home. As most dinner parties take place over the weekend, invitations stop once every one of her old clique learns of her out-of-town involvement. She still trains in her home gym, but with waning enthusiasm.

Pull yourself together, she thinks. *You can't let yourself go.* And she resolutely decides to join the local gym. The female changing rooms are deserted when Carla walks in to drop off her bag. The heavy weightlifting bars are stacked in a roofed area outside, with a welcome breeze keeping the temperature at a bearable level. As she assembles the heavy weight bar, a dark-blonde woman joins her. One look tells Carla that this woman is used to lifting heavier weights than she does.

"Hi. I'm Charlotte, or Lottie for short, mind if I join you? Maybe assist you in your heavier lifts.

"Hi Lottie, Carla. Yes, I would like that. I lift at home, but without any assistance. I play it safe and don't dare to push myself to the limit."

Lottie nods in agreement and takes up a position in front of Carla. "Sumo or dead lift?" she asks Carla.

"Dead," says Carla using an underhand grip outside her knees.

"Hollow back," Lottie corrects her.

Appreciating the other woman's no-nonsense approach and professional advice, Carla takes to Lottie instantly.

One hour later, the two women are sitting in the shade of a tree in the elevated cafeteria that overlooks the Olympic-size swimming pool.

"I am going to have a protein shake," says Lottie. "Do you care for one?"

"I made my recovery shake up at home, so I'm going to have a latte," Carla replies.

"Are you on holiday?" asks Lottie.

"No, I live here, but – as I said – I train at home. My best friend went back to her business of event planning in Cape Town, so I decided to give the gym a try. And you?"

"My dad lives here and on one of my visits I met up with a guy in the gym and decided to stick around to see how things worked out – no pun intended."

"And?" Carla smiles.

"So far so good." Lottie smiles back. "Until he got called to that mission, that is."

Not wanting to appear too nosey in their first encounter, Carla does not probe deeper.

"Are you married?" Lottie asks.

"Recently divorced, after over thirty years,' Carla says, sipping at her latte.

"Join the club," Lottie grimaces. "Half the women over fifty in this gym must be divorcees."

"You are kidding," Carla laughs.

"Stick around; see for yourself. Same time tomorrow?" Lottie asks while getting up.

"Sure, see you," Carla replies, taking the last couple of sips from her latte glass.

By the following Friday, their third, shared training session, Carla has Lottie's entire life-story.

Pregnant and married at 17; divorced by 22; second marriage and another daughter, both in Cape Town. Second divorce. Entered and won bodybuilding competitions before becoming a professional trainer. A verbal fight with her boss – the bastard would not have survived my first punch – and escape to Daddy for a while. Now Bruce, her latest hope, is on some type of military mission.

All that over three protein shakes after their workouts.

Jeez, who am I to complain? Carla thinks on her way to spend the weekend in P.E. *At least I didn't have any kids to worry about.*

"Why don't you come and spend a weekend with me for a change?" Carla suggests, stroking Micky's bare chest after their first hurried bout of love making.

"We would lose one night together," Mickey reckons, "as I would have to leave on Sunday afternoon. Four nights without you is bad enough," he adds pulling her on top of him.

Hm, what have I been missing all these years, she thinks, giving in to his demands, the subject all but forgotten for the time being.

"Have you heard from Bruce?" Carla asks on the following Tuesday morning as she and Lottie are warming up on the cross-trainer.

"Yes, he phoned me from London. He will be released after some kind of debriefing. He is going to transfer money into my account so that I can pay the rent at the holiday apartment we rented two months ago. How was your weekend? Judging by the lack of a tan, it rained in P.E."

Carla blushes and leads the way to the weightlifting section.

With her routine now firmly in place, Carla loses track of time until on one Tuesday afternoon she is disturbed by the ring of the intercom. Instead of the usual call from security at the complex entrance, it is at her side gate.

"Yes?" she replies, sorry not to have a camera at the gate. "Mrs Fowler?"

"Yes?"

"Constable Wepenaar, Police. May we talk to you?"

She opens the gate to see the policeman in front of her and a colleague leaning against a police van at the top of her driveway.

"We need you to come with us to the police station," says the policeman.

"What is it about?" Carla asks.

"We were asked to bring you in, that's all: no details," he shrugs.

"Give me a moment ..."

"Please, Mrs Fowler, just lock up and come with us, I am just following my orders."

Shrugging her shoulders Carla picks her bag off the hallway counter and locks the door. Opening the garage door with her remote control, she says: "Shall I follow you?"

"No, Madam, you are coming with us," he says, "you can close up your garage."

Unsteadily she walks up the driveway where the second policeman is holding open the back gate to the van.

"I am not getting in there," protests Carla.

"I am afraid you have to," says Constable Wepenaar, extending a hand to help her into the cage of the van, "there is only a place for me and the driver in the cab."

In the charge office at the local police station, the duty officer does not waste time in telling her what she needs to know.

"Missus Fowler, you are under arrest for contempt of court, please put your valuables and personal belongings into this safe box for us to keep until your release. You will appear in front of the magistrate tomorrow, or as soon as a court appearance can be arranged. Until then you will be held in custody in our police cell in the back of this complex."

"But, but, but ..."

Chapter Twenty-Six

Kent & Tanya

Taking advantage of the mild evening, their table has been laid on the veranda, covered with a lilac wisteria. "Ahmed," Ottmar calls to the young waiter who is serving them again, "please bring us a bottle of the *Cuvée Brut Felix Krull*, we have reason to celebrate."

"Who is Felix Krull?" asks Tanya, having some difficulty pronouncing the name.

Ottmar laughs: "A folly of mine. *The Confessions of Felix Krull* is an unfinished novel by the German author Thomas Mann about a confidence trickster, a novel I wish the author had finished. I named my *Cuvée Brut* 'Felix Krull' because it tricks you into believing it is from the Champagne region."

Ahmed ceremoniously uncorks the bottle with a trained 'pop' and pours the pale, effervescent liquid into crystal fluted glasses.

With a *"Zum wohl"*, *"Good health,"* and *"Prosit!"*, they clink their glasses and take a first, appreciative sip of the zero-alcohol, carbonated, vintage wine.

"Remarkable," Tanya comments, since she has enjoyed the odd glass of French Champagne in the past.

Ottmar inclines his head in satisfaction. "I hope you will continue with my legacy. The spinning-cone alcohol extraction technology is still in its infancy in this country but well worth developing. As you have already tasted, my results to date are very satisfying."

Their dinner of braised quail, served on a creamy mushroom polenta is further accompanied by a Pinotage Nought Reserve, which lingers on their palates even after they have indulged in an Italian affogato (an espresso gelato, or coffee topped with ice cream).

"So," Ottmar finally says, "why are you so interested in the hangar? Are you by any chance intending to build your own round-the-world yacht or trimaran?"

"Nothing of the kind," says Kent and lays out a vivid picture of their plans. Taking over from each other, as one runs out of breath, the couple literally ad-lib their plans in front of their host, who listens absolutely spellbound to their detailed projections.

"Good grief," Ottmar bursts out as they both stop, mentally spent by their vision.

"Looking at the two of you and listening to you, I believe that you will do it," says Ottmar. "Reserve me a seat for your première."

The following weeks are spent in taking over from Ottmar as the necessary securities are lodged to conclude the sale of the wine estate, inclusive of the adjacent tract of rocky gorge housing the large hangar.

To the couple's surprise, Ottmar virtually hands over the reins to them the moment he has spoken to his lawyer and received the bank's guarantees. He devotes most of his days and evenings to Kent and Tanya, taking time out when necessary to see to the transfer of his yacht, and mustering a crew for the sea trials. By common agreement, the guest house is closed "for renovations".

Late one night, after another exhausting day familiarising herself with the running of the wine farm. Tanya uses the couple's code-name for the hangar site to ask: "What's the next step '*across the road*'?"

"Your friend Jerry Jacobs in Australia has agreed to design the new insides of the hangar," Kent replies. "He says the dimensions are more than adequate. I think you should invite him to come over to familiarise himself with the scope of the project."

"Good idea," she murmurs with closed eyes, breathing softly in instant slumber.

Kent smiles to himself and gives his own thoughts free reign.

Am I mad to take on this venture? A wine farm of all places AND the project across the road – millions of hard-earned money over the last forty-five years on the line! Why don't I just pack a bag and travel the world? Look how much fun we had just travelling to the Maldives and through South Africa. Am I back on an ego trip?

No, he tells himself, *this is not just me. This time it is US! We want to do this together. But are we? Am I going to leave Tanya to look after the wine estate, while I develop the project across the road, which has really been her idea, and is based on her expertise?*

Am I not creating the very same situation that broke up my marriage to Carla: two people living their own lives, instead of supporting each other in one goal? Not only was I attracted to Hot Stuff by her extraordinary sensuality and looks, but by her projection of harmony: that seamless fusion of our common passion for music and for a life together as one.

Cradling a sleeping Tanya in his arms, he makes his final decision before allowing himself to doze off: *In the morning I will change this situation.*

"I think you know enough about the wine farm now," says Kent as they are getting dressed for breakfast. "I need your expertise on the project across the road. What do you think?"

"What? Do you expect me to manage the estate and help you?" she replies with uncharacteristic sharpness in her voice.

"No, my love," he quickly placates her, pulling her into his arms. "We are not wine farmers; nor do we want to be. We will get a manager and focus on what we are good at together."

Relief floods her face, coupled with a hint of her usual smile: "Thank you," she says, getting onto her toes to give him a lingering kiss.

"Hmmm," he sighs, but she pushes him away gently: "I am ravenous for breakfast: you will have to wait until tonight."

When Tanya and Kent join him on the veranda, Ottmar rises from the table.

"A full-house breakfast for me, please Ahmed," Tanya tells the young waiter as he pours her coffee. Kent sticks to his usual coffee and an almond croissant.

"I received an interesting call this morning," Ottmar says. "A young Myburgh, Jnr is looking for a job as a wine maker and farm manager. His parents own a large estate in Stellenbosch that the eldest son is running. Jannie feels underutilised over there, plus: he is very interested in my non-alcoholic wine technology, which his brother wants nothing to do with."

"That's quite a coincidence," Kent responds, "because we were going to ask you this very morning if you knew of somebody suitable to run the wine side of the business. Why don't you invite him for lunch or dinner?"

"It will have to be dinner," Ottmar says. "I am putting the last members of the crew together." He excuses himself to make the call to Jannie Myburgh, Jnr.

"Uncanny," says Kent, "we were only just talking about getting a manager, and there he is. Let's hope he is what we are looking for.

At six-thirty on the dot Ahmed escorts a freckle-faced, tousle-haired, young man onto the veranda, where the table is set for four. Jannie Myburgh is dressed in khaki pants, checked shirt, and scuffed suede *veldskoen*, or half-boots.

Over dinner, Jannie tells them of his upbringing on his father's wine farm, his agricultural college education, as well as his wine-farming and wine-making experience to date. At first addressing Ottmar, but soon being made aware of the German's imminent departure, he focuses his attention on the couple instead.

"What are your intentions for the estate?" he finally asks when he has completed his own repertoire.

Kent feels it's best to play down the project across the road for the time being and says: "Our main interest is in the music business. We are escaping from the city and hoping to lead a more community-oriented life in this beautiful part of the world."

Tanya continues: "We were drawn here by the description of a charming Cape Dutch homestead nestled among vineyards in the foothills of the Klein Drakenstein mountains. One look at the picture and we knew that we had to come here."

Kent adds: "Mister Ellerine's wish to get back onto the water, opened an unforeseen opportunity for us that we could not resist."

It is nearly midnight when Kent, Tanya, and Jannie shake hands on formalising a contract with the assistance of their lawyers.

"I like him," says Tanya after they have seen Jannie off.

Three weeks later, Jannie Myburgh, Junior, is officially appointed the winemaker and manager of the Klein Drakenstein Valley Estate. With his wife Annelise, who has been hired as the future manager of the guesthouse they intend to re-open once Kent and Tanya have moved across the road; when Jannie takes up residence in Ottmar's old quarters.

Chapter Twenty-Seven

Kent

Just after 4.30 am, the lights are switched on in Carla's cell and a policewoman tells her to get ready for breakfast in the anteroom to the charge office.

"What is happening?" asks a dishevelled Carla, who has just spent the worst night of her life in a cell in police custody. "You will be taken to appear in front of the magistrate in Humansdorp this morning," says the policewoman, placing a metal tray with some type of porridge, two slices of plain, brown bread, and a cup of black coffee in front of her. "Humansdorp?" and then it dawns on her. *The traffic fine I had received for speeding. The policeman had explained me: I could pay it within 30 days at the Humansdorp Traffic Department or defend myself in court at the stated date. Damn! What did I do with that fine notice? I stuffed it into the side pocket of my handbag, together with all my grocery receipts. My handbag? Shit! It was in Leonora's bag that I borrowed, and the bitch has taken the bag back with her to Cape Town, after leaving my purse, my lipstick, and my hairbrush on the dresser, but not the fine. Did Leonora do it intentionally? I wouldn't put it past her.*

"I don't drink coffee first thing in the morning. Can I have a cup of green tea instead?" she asks the policewoman who is keeping an eye on her from a chair next to the door.

"Where do you think you are, lady? The bloody Ritz Hotel? Green tea? Ha!" the woman snorts.

Less than fifteen minutes later, Carla is sitting on the back seat of a police car with an expanded-metal grid separating her from the driver and the policewoman. The safe box with her personal belongings on the seat between them is right in front of her.

"No pit stops," the policewoman announces. "You can go to the toilet when we get there."

Carla sits back and stares out of the barred window at the passing landscape she knows so well, having travelled this way twice a week.

Jeez, she thinks, *what is happening to me?"* she thinks. *When will my life return to normal? What is normal? Ever since I sold my hair salon and moved down to the Cape coast, I have had nothing but bad luck: husband gone after forty years together; Hennie gone; Lex gone; best friend gone. How long before Micky is gone too?*

Uncontrollable sobs shake her body.

What am I doing with my life? I never had time for hobbies really: just work, the dogs, and my home gym. Should I sell up and move to PE to be closer to Micky? And do what? Or should I go to Denmark and live with my clever, spinster sister? Shit, shit, shit – how have I deserved all this? Why?

"Okay, out you come," says the policewoman as the police car comes to a stop at the back door of the Humansdorp magistrate court building.

In the courtroom, she is ushered into a row of seats with four other women. She is the only one in cut-off jeans, a crumpled, smelly tank-top, sandals, and streaks of blond tresses hanging over her face.

Why did the cops not give me a chance to get dressed properly? Surely they must have known what lay in store for me.

The morning drags along with case after case being deliberated and dealt with by the elderly magistrate. Shortly before lunch, Carla's case is called up: failure to pay a traffic fine with the option of contesting the fine in court having expired.

The magistrate looks with a wry smile at Carla. "It appears to me," he intones, "that the law-enforcement officers did not give you much of a chance to prepare yourself for this hearing."

"No, my Lord, they did not," Carla blurts out. "They just knocked on my door, took me to the police station, locked me up for the night, and brought me here this morning."

"You spent the night in jail?"

"Yes, your Honour," says Carla, remembering the way judges were addressed in courtroom dramas on television.

The magistrate looks at her again. "Are you prepared to pay the fine?"

"Of course, your Honour. Somehow the piece of paper ended up between my grocery receipts and was overlooked."

The magistrate scribbles on a piece of paper before proclaiming:

"The court upholds the charge and instructs that the fine ought to be paid in full by the close of business today. The defendant has been absolved of her alternative prison sentence and is free to go."

Carla bursts into tears of relief. "Thank you, your Honour, she exclaims, but the magistrate is already rising, after having announced a lunch break, without reference to her gratitude.

After she paid the fine at the Humansdorp Traffic Department, the drive back to her house, is spent in silence, apart from the insistent squawks of the police radio.

At the top of her driveway, the policewoman opens the back door of the police sedan from the outside, and steps aside to let Carla get out. Bending back into the front compartment, the woman retrieves the safe box, returns Carla's belongings, and makes her sign a receipt. Without so much as a "Goodbye", but with just a nod of the head, the policewoman gets back into the car, and they drive off.

Later lying in an exhausted state in a steaming, oil-scented tub with a mug of green tea resting on the tiles beside her, Carla is relieved the ordeal is over.

"Where have you been?" asks Lottie when Carla joins her at the heavyweight's rack on the following morning.

"Would you believe it, if I told you that I have been in police custody?" Carla replies.

"You? In jail? Let's go and have a coffee or a shake: I must hear this." Lottie insists on picking up her sports bag, instead of leaving it in the locker. "All my personals are in there, if they get stolen, I am stuffed," she had confided to Carla.

"I don't believe it!" Lottie exclaims when Carla has finished telling her story. "Do you think your friend Leonora did it on purpose?" she asks.

"No, I don't think so," Carla replies. "I phoned her last night and she sounded genuinely shocked; said she just upended all the shopping receipts into the rubbish bin without checking."

With that subject closed, Carla says: "What's happening with you and Bruce?"

Lottie puffs up her cheeks and expels a blast of air: "Phew! I got tossed out of the holiday flat," she scowls. "The money transfer never came through to pay the bill. I am back with my dad, who is driving me crazy, treating me like a blinking teenager. I think I will go back and stay with my daughter, to look after my grandchildren until I figure what to do next."

"Hey, sorry to hear that," says Carla. "Shall we go and train?"

Fifteen minutes later, they both realise that their hearts are not in it and decide to go for a pizza instead.

"Comfort food," they console themselves and order a carafe of House Red to share.

Chapter Twenty-Eight

Kent & Tanya

With his hands lodged firmly in the back pocket of his blue jeans, Jerry Jacobs stands in the wide-open doors of the hangar. "Perfect," he says, scanning the steel-gabled roof high above the three of them. "Wide enough for the inner and outer studio with loads of room for a mezzanine floor."

He opens his laptop on a large trestle-table to show them his virtual reality CAD layout. "Sound-proof studio in the left half of the hangar," he explains. "The right side we can break down into an iso-booth for solo recordings, and the actual recording and mixing equipment studio. Then we have a small kitchen, toilets, and so on, with a spiral staircase leading up to your quarters, which will include an open-plan kitchen; a bedroom; and large floor-to-ceiling glass sliders for a front-row view of the stage below, the Amphitheatre, and the Klein Drakenstein Mountains. I envy you guys already."

Kent replies: "Very impressive. If we start with the wooden crossbeams for the mezzanine, we can hang the sound-proofing ceiling for the studio off it, giving you and Tanya space and time for downstairs, while I finish off our quarters and move us in."

"I can't wait," says Tanya. "How long before we can move in?"

"Four to six weeks, I guess," says Kent. "The timber won't be a problem, but it will depend on where the triple-glazed sliding doors and windows will be coming from."

"Talking about glass," says Jerry, "apart from what we need in your loft and between the studios, what have you got in mind for the outside of the hangar to make it look more presentable to the public?"

Kent scratches his short-cropped hair and says: "The hangar look will have to go. We need to open in front and around the two long sides for parking, which will double as a firebreak. The rear, facing the Amphitheatre and the mountains, will get the stage with a widescreen for video projections, while the hidden entrance to the interior will take care of itself. Have you got something in mind, Jerry?"

"I have," the Australian replies. "The two long sides could be clad with a stone wall built from locally sourced rock to match the backdrop of the mountain. The masonry will slope at forty-five degrees from the mountain side down to the road. The remaining triangles and the entire front should be black, reflective glass, mirroring the sky on the sides and the vineyards across the road."

"Brilliant Jerry," Tanya applauds as she visualises the dramatic effect.

"Stunning," Kent agrees, since he is familiar with glass facade structures and their appeal from downtown Johannesburg.

While Jerry and Tanya busy themselves with the final design of the studios and the building's exterior, Kent contacts local contractors to visit the site and prepare quotations. *This time I am not budging for one minute from this site until we are done*, he thinks, remembering only too well how the house on the Cape coast, now Carla's house, had gone so horribly wrong in his absence.

Two weeks later, Jerry Jacobs leaves for Australia with the promise to return the moment they need him.

"What name have you in mind for this venture?" asks Ron Edwards, who is once again Kent's corporate lawyer.

"We don't want mixed identities," Kent replies. "The wine estate and this project will be two entirely separate businesses. The moment we move out of our room in the guesthouse Jannie Myburgh Junior will be in sole command. Quite confidentially, I have a feeling his old man will buy the estate for him to avoid conflict between the brothers in the future."

"That would suit you nicely, if the price is right," says Ron.

Tanya leans across the table. "The name we have chosen has a double *entendre*; it is made up from parts of our first names, and hints at our core business of recording music: '*taKeOne*'" she smiles.

"Do you want me to register the name?" Ron asks.

"You may have to add '*studio*' or '*records*'," says Kent. "See what is available."

The building work gets off to a quick start. The carpenters who had helped restore Ottmar Ellerine's yacht are not only keen to undertake the substantial construction of the mezzanine and the studios, but also secure all the necessary timber at discounted prices. As is often the case in small communities, by word of mouth, stone masons, a plumber, and an electrician come to offer their services to Kent.

The stage at the back of the hangar is completed first, followed by the mezzanine floor and intricate spiral staircase. The cladding that will need to be removed to make way for the mezzanine's sliding doors is cut out after a full-length veranda has been built that also serves as the roof and ceiling of the stage. Through this opening the carpenters can now hoist all the timber and cladding they need to complete Kent and Tanya's loft apartment.

"Do you think we can have a bathtub near the window, as well as a shower in this bathroom?" asks Tanya one evening after inspecting the day's progress with Kent.

"Only if you promise to close the curtains," he grins.

"Don't be daft, it's one-way, reflective glass: no one will be able to see me, even if a spotlight is shining on me," she says.

"Well, then you will have a bathtub," he promises.

The glazing contractor comes to inspect the build when the stonemasons have finished their task, to check the final measurements of the reflective glass. "This is some place you are building here, Mister Fowler," he says. "When is the grand opening?"

"Only when we are one hundred percent sure that everything is perfect," Kent replies.

Jerry Jacobs is back from Australia six month later. "My goodness, guys! What have you done? What a transformation, not an inch of the old hangar is visible. The reflective glazing just bounces the whole gorge back at you. Do I see solar panels on the roof? It's a bloody fairy tale come true, mate: I can't wait to get inside."

After a quick walk around, he settles down and checks how Tanya has managed with the help of a local sound engineer. "Great job," says Jerry," I like the heavy, black curtains in the studio: the sound quality is excellent in all ranges and easy to adjust in any area we want by shifting the curtain."

With Kent and Tanya's loft now completed and closed in by glazing, Jerry comes up for the first time to have a look around. "Holy bloody moly, guys!" he exclaims, taking in the view of the Klein Drakenstein mountains framing the vast expanse of glass.

Behind a panelled partition, a door allows access to the heavily insulated ceiling of the sound studio below. "That's great, if we need to lay more cables or simply need to store stuff."

On the following morning, Jerry takes a guitar to the small iso-booth studio, after telling Tanya to do a single-track recording. The result is excellent.

"What have you got lined up for me in the big studio?" he asks Tanya.

"Word has got around in the local community," Tanya replies that the old hangar is now a recording studio. The other day a group of farmworkers came and gave me a tape of a song they recorded at a local hall: their version of Marvin Gaye's 'I Heard It Through The Grapevine.' I played around with it and came up with quite a good re-mix."

"Let's hear it," Jerry demands. After listening to it twice over, he says: "Their recording is bloody terrible, but these voices and your treatment sure makes a man sit up. Can we get the buggers in here, coach them, and record them in our studio? Then you can re-mix the high-quality recording to see what you can squeeze out of it. What do you think, Hot Stuff?"

Kent and Tanya burst out laughing: "It's been a while since someone called me 'Hot Stuff', don't you think, Rooster?"

"It does sound strange. Does it still fit?" Kent grins and promptly lets out his famous crow.

"Who is the lead-singer?" asks Tanya, looking at the motley group of seven seated on the floor of the outdoor stage.

"We are," says a tall girl in her twenties, dressed in dungarees over a colourful, short-sleeve shirt, her dark hair tied back with a bandana, Tanya can see that this young woman spends her days outdoors.

"It's like so, Miss," the younger woman says. "We don't have any instruments when we work with the vines, so we *jes' sommer* sing: one starts a song, and the others join in." In order to demonstrate, she sings in a clear, strong voice: "*Is this the real life? Is this just fantasy? Caught in a landslide, no escape from reality,*" with the others joining in perfect harmony.

The backdoor to the stage is pushed open by Jerry so hard, banging against the stage wall, that the small group stop abruptly.

"'Bohemian Rhapsody'! Who the bloody hell is singing 'Bohemian Rhapsody' out here?" he demands.

Tanya points at the little group. "They are: isn't it beautiful?" she says.

"It gave me frigging goose bumps," says Jerry, before addressing the group. "On that demo you had background music?"

"*Ja, Meneer,*" says the tall girl. "We used a karaoke backtrack. We don't normally do that, but we thought it would sound better."

"Listen here ..." says Jerry. "What's your name?"

"It's Estella, *Meneer* ..."

"Listen here, Estella: stick to singing and leave the thinking to us. Come inside; we will put you in the sound studio and talk you through the procedure."

Less than half an hour later, the group of four girls and three males, each wearing wireless headphones, are standing nervously under the low lights of the sound studio, listening to Tanya's calm instructions.

"Estella," she says, "you start and then let the others fall in as you always do, each singing a different backing-instrument track. I will phase Estella's voice to your headphones so that you have her lead to follow. Wait for my countdown from three: 'three, two, one, go.'" Confused at first, they miss their cues three times before Tanya is happy to let them complete the song.

"Great," says Tanya. "Come by tomorrow after work to listen what the re-mix sounds like but, before you go, write your names down for me so that we know who's who."

Chatting excitedly, the seven farmworkers hand back the headphones and the list with their names: "*Estella, Lizzy, Abby, Gwyn, Jacob, Mannie, Luke.*

"What do you think?" says Tanya to Jerry who has been listening to the recording with his own headphones.

"It's good, but they need coaching to overcome their nerves. I bet you they are better in the fields."

"Hey, give them a break: this is their first time in a sound booth," Tanya protests.

"Okay, okay, keep your shirt on," Jerry concedes "but the voice of that Estella is something else. I have an idea I want to discuss with her tomorrow night."

Just after five-thirty on the following late afternoon, Tanya plays her re-mix to Kent and Jerry. They all agree: It's good, but disappointing.

The seven farmworkers listen a couple of times, before admitting that they need a lot more practise.

"Yes, definitely," says Jerry, "but there is something else. I want to pull Estella out: she has the wrong voice for the rest of you. Let a male voice sing the lead."

A visibly distraught Estella is about to protest when Jerry asks her if she knew each track of the song in isolation. At first confused, she says after a moment's thought: "Yes, I think so, because we take turns with the lead." Jerry takes her to the iso-booth and explains what he wants her to do: "Slow the song down to the tempo of a ballad without lowering your voice. Sing each track following on your own lead and then we will feed you through your headphones."

Two-and-a-half hours' later, Tanya has ten tracks in front of her. Working through the night, she layers the tracks until she is happy, and the finished re-mix is sensational. Estella's clear, strong lead is blended expertly with her own soft, harmonious backing.

"My goodness!" Jerry exclaims, "I honestly did not expect that."

When they play it back to Estella later that afternoon, she bursts into tears of joy; spontaneously throwing her arms around Jerry. "Thank you!" she bursts out. "Thank you so much! May I have a copy for home?"

"What are you going to do with it?" asks Kent after listening to the recording.

"I have a DJ mate on one of the late-night stations in Oz. I'm going to ask the bugger to plug it."

"Great," Kent replies, "but make sure you have her sign a release agreement before you do."

Chapter Twenty-Nine

Carla

Carla pulls into Micky's driveway as he is lifting the last of his shopping bags out of the boot of his Audi. Having listened repeatedly on the phone about her contempt-of-court ordeal, he is somewhat relieved to see that she has regained her composure.

"Hi," he says cheerfully, trying to make light of the matter. "Did you go through any speed traps coming here?"

She gives him a filthy look and spits: "Easy for you to be smug, you take the easy way out; wait for me here in P.E. instead of offering to do the trip each weekend."

"Hold it," he counters. "I don't want to be in your home or your town. I happen to like it here just fine."

"And I like my home and my town just fine, and have had enough of running after you to do your things."

"Oh, yes? My things? Aren't you the one that can't get into the sack fast enough?"

Her slap hits him square on the left ear and before he has a chance to avoid it, the follow up hits him on the right side of his face.

"Stop it," he hisses, grabbing both her wrists. "Don't you dare hit me you, you ..."

Carla howls, trying to wrench free.

As his grip tightens in trying to force her to stop, she brings up her knee to connect full force with his groin. Stepping around his body as he lies doubled-up on the ground, she grabs her things, and reverses out of the still-open driveway gates.

Near hysterical, with tears of rage and frustration coursing down her face, she heads for the freeway to the west.

At the next lay-by, she pulls off the freeway and speed dials Micky's number.

No reply.

When it goes to voice mail she says: "I'm so sorry, Micky, I don't know what came over me. Sorry, it was all too much for me. I'm really, really, sorry. Please phone me."

Carla spends the weekend in her own bed, sleeping, watching TV, phoning Micky's number over and over without response. By Monday, her mind is made up: she is not going to run after him. Let him stew; he will come around eventually.

"Theresa, what a surprise! I am normally the one to phone you," says Carla to her older sister a week later.

"It's mother," her sister cries, "she collapsed and is in hospital. They put her in the intensive care unit. Father is with her. It doesn't look good. Can you come over?"

"Oh, Theresa, that is terrible! 'Course I'll come over. Give me a couple of days to get booked and organised. I'll phone you once I have spoken to the travel agent. Give my love to Mum and Father. Bye."

"Kent, it's me," says Carla when her ex-husband answers the phone.

"Hello Carla, can I phone you back? I am just in the middle of something."

"Kent, you have been in the middle of something or other for the last thirty-odd years. Just listen for one minute, please. Mum is in intensive care. Theresa tells me it's not looking good. I am flying to Denmark as soon as I can get a flight. Can I give the security company your number in case of an emergency?"

"Sure, Carla," Kent replies. "I am very sorry to hear about Mum. How are you for cash?"

"I'm okay, not to worry. I will keep you updated, Bye."

"Go well. Take care, Carla," she hears him say as she disconnects the call.

That's a first, she thinks. *He always hung up without hearing me out.*

Twenty-four hours' later she is perched on an Economy Class seat to Copenhagen, Denmark.

At Copenhagen's International airport, a crying Theresa throws her arms around Carla: "You are too late, Carla: Mum passed away last night, while you were in the plane. They sedated Father and are keeping him isolated for observation."

Driving through the busy early morning traffic to the clinic, Theresa says: "What are we going to do with Papa? We can't let him live by himself; not for a while anyway, until he adjusts. I have to work …"

Before she can finish the sentence, however, her younger sister interrupts her. "I'll look after Papa …"

"But you live in South Africa: what about your house …?"

"I am staying!" says Carla resolutely as they find parking at the small clinic.

"Papa, Papa, I am so sorry; I am so, so sorry," cries Carla pulling her frail, forlorn-looking father into the crock of her neck.

"Ah, Carla …" he sobs, "at least you are here."

With his two daughters by his side, a new energy seems to flow through Christian's veins. "When can I get out of here?" he demands. "Carla, you must come and stay with me; Theresa's place is too small, and she is forever working."

Looking at each other, the sisters say unanimously: "Yes, Papa!"

The doctor takes one look at Christian Carstens and turns to the sisters: "It would be good if at least one of you can stay with him for a while. Sometimes delayed shock can be devastating for an elderly person."

"I'll be staying with him," Carla re-assures the doctor, "and my sister is close by. He will be fine."

Since Carla has never been to the new apartment which their parents had rented in Copenhagen to be closer to Theresa, her sister accompanies Carla to the third-floor two-bed apartment.

"Make yourself at home," Theresa says, while Christian busies himself in the kitchen with the kettle and green tea bags which he knows his daughters prefer to coffee.

Every day, Christian tests Carla's resolve by asking without fail: "How long are you going to stay?"

"Papa, as I told you yesterday, I am staying for good. I am not going back to South Africa. I have had enough. Maybe things will work out better for me in Denmark, if Theresa is anything to go by."

To prove her point, she makes no bones about her calls to South Africa: "Hi Leonora, how are you?" Without waiting for a reply, she continues, "You still got the key for the house and remember the security code, right? … Good, I would like you to do something for me."

As an afterthought she asks: "You're still together with Brenda, right? ... Great, I am happy for you," she interjects, before adding: "Why don't the two of you enjoy a holiday in my home, while you get a removal company and pack up all my personal belongings and ship them to Denmark."

No longer able just to listen, Leonora blurts out: "Ship them to Denmark? Carla, are you on some kind of mind-altering substance?"

"Nothing of the kind," says Carla. "My mother has passed away, and I am staying here to look after my father."

"So sorry, Carla. How can I help?"

"Go and stay there while you pack up my things. Help yourself to whatever piece of furniture you and Brenda may find useful. No permanent fittings that form part of the house."

"What about your Mercedes Estate?" Leonora asks hopefully.

"You can buy it at its market value, if you have the cash."

"I'll speak to Brenda: she's the one with the money."

"Lucky you," retorts Carla, getting slightly exasperated with Leonora's gall.

"Your Honda?"

"Do you think you or Brenda can ride it?" Carla chortles.

"No, I mean, what do you want us to do with it?"

"I will let Kent know. He will have a buyer for it."

"Maybe he will give it to his sweetheart as a wedding present," Leonora can't help saying.

"Is he getting married?" says Carla before realising she has fallen for the barb. *She is such a bitch! How did I ever put up with her?* she thinks. "I will WhatsApp you my shipping details and you can give the removers my contact details so that I can pay them directly. Send me a WhatsApp if you think of anything else."

Then Carla phones Kent and, after telling him of her plans, he says: "Leave it with me, I will get Thomas and Ron onto it. They have your bank details here in SA, but you will have to organise the international transfer. Your bank will help you with that. Regards to Christian and Theresa, let me know if I can assist further."

"When is the wedding?" she can't help herself asking. But in his usual fashion he has already disconnected from her call.

"Sounds like you mean it," says her father.

"Yes, Papa, I mean it; I am going to stay with you."

Christian looks at her hesitantly before working up the courage to ask: "Do you think between the two of us we could manage to find a place a bit further up the Baltic seacoast? Your mother insisted on Copenhagen to be close to Theresa, but I hate it here, I hate the city and I miss the coast."

Carla remembers how her father had described his early life in the small rural harbour town of Faxe Ladeplads in Zealand just 60 kilometres south of Copenhagen. How vividly he described the scene of the elders sitting in the sun outside the grocers with their daily shopping of fresh bread, cheeses, and fish on Fridays, puffing on their pipes before returning to their respective homes.

"Is that what you want Papa? Sit on the sidewalk and yack about the good old days?" She smiles for the first time since her arrival.

"Maybe … I don't know if they would accept such a young man."

Not catching on, Carla admonishes him. "Papa, you are 88 years' old! Of course they will …" Seeing the glint in his eyes, however, she can't help laughing. "You had me there, Papa. Yes, let's take a train ride to Faxe, once we know how much we have in the bank between us."

Theresa, who has made all the funeral arrangements, can't believe her ears when she hears of their plans. Calming her down, Christian says solemnly: "Your mother would have wanted it that way!"

The small room in the funeral home is quiet as a young parson reads from the scriptures. Unfamiliar with the deceased, who had lived abroad in southern Africa most of her life, he keeps the eulogy neutral, extolling on Anna Carstens virtues as a caring wife and loving mother. Grateful for the simplicity of the service Christian, Theresa and Carla join the parson in the final prayer before committing the body for cremation.

Over lunch in a quiet backstreet restaurant, they reminisce over the family's life on the East Rand in South Africa. By the time the elderly waiter serves them dessert, the conversation has moved on to their plans for the next couple of days.

Not out to deter them, but rather to caution her father's expectations, Theresa says: "Fader, when were you last in Faxe Ladeplads?"

Scratching his head Christian says "In 1952," – as if it were yesterday.

The sisters exchange meaningful glances before Theresa continues: "Papa, that's over seventy years ago. Maybe the place has changed a little."

Carla, who has Googled Faxe Ladeplads, says: "2021 population: two thousand, eight hundred and seventy-four inhabitants; with those numbers I don't think a lot has changed since Fader's last visit."

Transferring to the local bus service outside the deserted Faxe railway station, Carla is pleased to see her father's growing excitement. I hope he won't be disappointed coming back after so many years, she thinks. But this is Denmark: like many other Scandinavian villages, little has changed.

They find a B&B one street back from the promenade leading to the small harbour and a new, large marina, half filled with sailing boats and larger live-on-board yachts. On either side of the marina and adjacent port, sand beaches stretch over to acres of pine forests that extend as far as the eye can see.

"This is beautiful, Papa," says Carla, "no wonder you liked coming here."

Walking in the shade of the tree-lined promenade, a couple of afternoons later, they both see a sign which reads:

To Let: Shop with apartment.

Enquire First Floor, Studio Solhavn

An open door leads to a worn, wooden stairway. Resolutely, Carla gestures to her father to follow her upstairs.

Turned away from a wide-open window, with the light falling over his shoulder, a dishevelled man in his fifties is seated in front of an easel, paintbrush momentarily suspended in mid-stroke.

"Can I help you?" he asks, his eyes straying appreciatively to Carla's cascading, flaxen tresses; her toned arms and muscular shoulders.

Used to evoking such an artist's reaction, Carla says: "We saw the sign in the window and are curious to see what is on offer."

"You are not from here," says the painter, placing his brush into a container, and wiping his hands on a piece of cloth that is sticking out of his left-hand pocket, "I can hear an accent. Pablo," he introduces himself with a quick smile. "Like in Picasso – I wish," he adds. "Let's go back downstairs and I will show you the shop, which is a bit narrow and small, because of the staircase to my studio. It used to be just a passage before I glassed it in to display my paintings. Alas! It does not work: My kind of art needs a little more space for the viewer to stand back and admire, so I decided to let the space with the apartment that goes off the courtyard."

Carla's expert eyes calculate the space she would require in front of a wall mirror and behind the hairdresser's chair. The two-bedroom apartment is in near darkness until Pablo throws open the windows and slatted shutters.

"One bathroom, a separate toilet, a kitchen, and a small living-room leading to the enclosed, cobbled courtyard: that would do the two of us, wouldn't it?" says Christian, taking in what is on offer.

Pablo smiles at him: "What have you got in mind for the small shop? It isn't much I am afraid, and barely enough space for a couple of chairs on the sidewalk."

Christian pulls his worn leather wallet out of his back-pocket and extracts an old photograph. This is my Carla with her gold medal at the World Hairdressing Championship in California, US of A. She knows what this space is good for, believe me."

"Papa, how do you know?"

"I may be old, but I am not stupid. I saw your eyes taking in the measurements as we walked through to have a look at the apartment."

Pablo looks at the photo and then at Carla with renewed interest.

"World champion hairdresser, heh? We could do with one," he grins, running a paint-stained hand through his unruly shock of grey-blond locks.

Carla laughs at him, "Your trim would be on the house."

"How could I refuse an offer from such a charming lady?" he

says, looking into her brown eyes, as she feels a blush creeping up her cheeks.

Is this for real? she thinks. *We haven't even got here!*

Chapter Thirty

Kent & Tanya

"Someone wants to see you over here in my office," says Jannie Myburgh, when Kent answers the crow of his smart phone.

"Now?" asks Kent checking the time. *Six-thirty? The tasting room has been closed for over an hour*, he thinks. "Be right over," he says.

"Please bring Tanya as well," he hears Jannie add, on someone's muted request.

"Okay."

The resemblance is unmistakable to Kent and Tanya when they enter the winemaker's office minutes later.

"Sorry to but in on you unannounced," says Jan Myburgh, Senior, who has risen to greet them. "Jan is the name. Do you mind if I call you Tanya and Kent?'"

They shake hands and take seats on opposing settees in front of an old, beautifully restored fireplace.

"Tanya, Kent," the older Myburgh begins, "I have been following your progress with great interest. Without having been close enough to admire your attention to detail, I am more than pleased to see the transformation of that ghastly boat hangar: a real eyesore in this beautiful countryside." Kent and Tanya both laugh in agreement. "I couldn't wait for that Ellerine to finish his yacht and bugger off." While they continue to smile at Myburgh's lack of candour, he laughs at their amusement and continues:

"I offered to buy him out several times," he says, "but he turned me down, saying that he needed to finish that yacht and his non-alcoholic experiments first. Your timing must have been perfect, and then – to my and my son's surprise – you are not even interested in the estate but promptly employ my youngest son and devote yourself to that project across the road. Tell me, what's going on?"

For the next half hour, Tanya and Kent take turns, as usual, in laying out their long term vision.

As they are talking, they can see Jan Senior sitting up and move forward on the settee. "Amazing, absolutely amazing!" he exclaims. "And, to crown it all, no one can hear a thing – totally sound-proof. Less disturbing than the local community dances."

"Yes," Kent confirms, "but you will be able to hear the open-air concerts. Although the gorge behind the natural amphitheatre will swallow up most of it."

"How many concerts are you planning?" asks Jan.

"One a month, we hope," Tanya replies. "We hope to attract top artists to record with us and to perform at the same time to sponsor our community charities. You see, Jan, we are registering a no-for-profit charity organisation."

"I admire your cause. Heaven knows this area needs it," says Myburgh. "Well, let me say two things," he continues. "One: my wife and I will come to each and every one of your concerts; and Two: would my buying this wine estate for Jannie Junior help you with your plans?"

Kent looks Jan squarely in the eye and says: "The wine estate, minus 'the property across the road', as we refer to it."

"Fair enough: it's of no use to us, anyway," Myburgh agrees. "One more question: will Jannie, Junior, have a free hand to do as he sees fit, as he has with me?"

Myburgh puts his right hand on his heart and says: "So help me God."

"In that case I am happy to have a look at an offer," says Kent.

"You will have my offer within forty-eight hours."

"Thank you. I look forward to welcoming you personally at our concerts."

The two men shake hands as Tanya and Jannie Junior hug each other.

With only the moon and thousands of stars in the sky that night, the Klein Drakenstein Mountains are bathed in a silvery light in front of Kent and Tanya as they sit on the balcony of their loft, breathing in the cool air.

"Well," Tanya murmurs, "that was an unexpected turn of events."

"Yes, indeed," Kent agrees, "and a welcome one: not just for the money, but for the freedom to focus on our project entirely."

That afternoon, Jerry receives the news from Estella, who has "heard it through the grapevine" from Ahmed's wife, who had been eavesdropping in turn on the vintner couple's conversation over breakfast.

"Come, I want to show you my favourite place," Estella says after Jerry has switched off the microphone in the iso-booth, where they are recording yet another track for Estella's forthcoming debut album.

Emerging through the stage door into the bright afternoon sun, Jerry is momentarily blinded. "Blimey, it's bloody hot outside!" he says, following Estella down the steps into the expanse of the amphitheatre. It has come to no one's surprise that Jerry and Estella have become 'an item', considering the amount of time they have been spending together in the studio. While she is in awe of his expertise, he is smitten by her voice, her looks, and her bright, quick-witted intellect which matches perfectly his brash, Aussie sense of humour.

Making their way up the gorge, she follows a narrow path next to a clear, tumbling brook. Less than two hundred metres up the slope, they come to an overhang of grey rock, partially shading a level plateau. Off to one side, the brook they have been following tumbles over rocks into a crystal-clear pool. Not wasting a moment, Estella strips down to her flimsy, bikini underwear and wades resolutely into the cool mountain water.

Jerry strips down to his boxers and splashes in after her.

Pulling her lithe body to him, he gently turns in the water until they both face the clearing under the overhang of solid rock. Pointing ahead, Jerry says: "This is where we are going to build our house."

"You can't build a house here," Estella pouts, "you are going to destroy the land."

Jerry smiles: "Sorry, baby, I meant a tent that can be erected and taken down."

"I am not going to live in a tent, that you have to crawl in and out of like a mole," she protests.

Now Jerry is laughing, visualising the image. "I'll show you later, on my laptop. The tent is similar to what the old people used to build in the Northern Cape, the *matjieshuis*. This one is from Asia and is called a 'yurt'. But it's closer in shape to the *indlu* or 'hut' of the traditional amaXhosa people, because it has a low wall made from a lattice of woodwork and then a small lattice dome is placed on top with the whole thing covered with skins or felt."

"*Nee wat*," Estella complains, "I am not sure I would like that. I would rather like a proper house with a table and chairs ..."

Jerry interrupts her: "You will have all that, my darling, and much more besides. It will be better than a five-star hotel, believe me. Let me show you before you condemn it."

"Oh, alright," she brightens up, and then – remembering the gossip she had been told by Ahmed's wife – she blurts out: "Did Kent tell you that he sold the wine farm?"

"Don't talk rubbish," he says dropping her into the water. Spluttering for air, Estella surfaces and coughs before adding: "the wine farm, but not the land this side of the road."

Jerry sighs a breath of relief: "Good riddance, now we only have one project to deal with. I bet he got a good deal, otherwise he would not have sold."

They let the sun dry them off, while Jerry continues to extol the merits of living here with her.

"What's this I hear, mates?" asks Jerry when he sees Tanya and Kent on the following day, "You sold the wine farm?"

Kent nods: "Just the wine estate, we keep this side of the road." Jerry says.

"I bet you did alright then?"

"Yes, we did. Ellerine was so eager to get away, he sold to us at a depressed-market value. Now that things are picking up again, we got the full price plus a handsome bonus to help pay for the studio."

"How far does your property actually go?" Jerry asks nonchalantly, not wanting to pre-empt his next question.

"Some five hundred-odd metres up the mountain," Kent replies.

"Do you think I could build myself a little yurt a bit away from the amphitheatre?" Jerry asks.

"A Yurt?" Tanya chimes in. "One of those Mongolian tents?"

"That's it," says Jerry, pleased that she at least knows what he is talking about.

More for Estella's than Kent and Tanya's benefit, Jerry has put together a video of modern-day yurts that are becoming fashionable all over the world as a form of quick-to-build alternate housing.

"Hey," Kent agrees, "that is ingenuous. What are the dimensions?"

"Off the peg, ready-to-assemble models are available in five-, seven-, nine- and twelve- metre diameters," Jerry replies, "with a ceiling height of five metres. Some even have a mezzanine, like your loft in the studio building."

"What size would you choose for yourself?" asks Tanya.

Jerry shifts around on his seat for a moment before admitting: "It's not just going to be for me: I am going to marry Estella."

Although aware of their relationship, the permanence of his statement takes them both by surprise.

"Does she know?" asks Tanya.

"Well, sort of: we sort of considered it, but I don't think she took me seriously."

Kent laughs, remembering his father's advice many years ago, when he had said: "The male weaverbird builds his nest, twig by twig, weaving it into a dome to lure his wife," so he says out loud: "Maybe you must get weaving to woo your female."

A couple of days later, Jerry presents Kent with the blueprint of his yurt.

"Run me through it and convince me that this is going to work on the place you have chosen," says Kent, playing the Devil's advocate role.

"Okay," says Jerry, taking a deep breath. "The yurt is constructed of a wooden trellis, one, point-five metres high. The trellis is the expanded to form a circle. I have chosen a nine-metre diameter, which fits comfortably into the clearing under the natural rock overhang. There are no signs of rockfall in that clearing."

"Better have a geotechnical engineer check it out," suggests Kent.

The Aussie nods, making a note on his blueprint, before continuing.

"A lattice dome is erected on top of the trellis, much like the spokes of a large umbrella, and tied with thin ropes to the trellis. That's the skeleton; the cover will consist of a strong UV resistant PVC tarpaulin as now used on long-haul truck-trailers, tailored to fit over the wooden skeleton like a tight bathing-cap."

"So far, so good," says Kent, "I see there is a door and windows."

"Yes, a wooden door with polycarbonate panels for extra light. The windows will also have opaque, polycarbonate panes for a soft light inside."

"All sounds great so far. What about the floor and ventilation?"

"In a common yurt, packed earth is used as flooring," says Jerry, "but, if we want to reduce the ecological footprint of the building and its impact on the environment, were we to take the yurt down, I want to use a wooden platform resting on four or five supports."

"Explain ..." Kent says by way of encouragement.

The shelf consists of boulders and softer sandstone, with deep pockets of decomposed rock, thousands of years old, I reckon. We could determine where the pillars ought to go and then drive thick iron rods maybe half a metre into the ground to secure a collection of 500 x 500 x 500 high pillars, onto which we can then secure our wooden platform – the floor of the yurt."

"Nice," says Kent, "it will look like the whole deck is floating."

"Fair dinkum," the Aussie enthuses, "and with the dome of the yurt on it, the whole thing will look like a flying saucer from outer space."

"Fantastic!" Kent exclaims, "but what about ventilation?"

"Yurts traditionally have an opening with a cap in the top to let smoke from their cooking fires escape. I am planning on a polycarbonate hood, suspended high enough to let the hot air out. Vents in the periphery of the floorboards will suck in the cold air and push the hot air out of the top. Most efficient, free air-conditioning one can get," says Jerry beaming with enthusiasm.

"Services?" says Kent, going into every detail of the proposal.

"For sewerage: we lay the necessary pipe into a trench we dig with a ditch-witch, fill in after the pipe is tested for leaks and plant over. Same with an electrical cable from the battery-wall of the studio's solar roof. I'll put a smaller battery-wall in the yurt, that can charge small appliances during the day.

"And last, but not least, we have lovely clean mountain water right on our doorstep. I'll divert some of it into a well and pull it up with a small pump into a feeder tank which we will hide behind the five-metre-high yurt."

"Looks to me like you got it all worked out," says Kent, "who is going to build it?"

"The same team we used for the woodwork of the studio and your loft," says Jerry.

"When will you start?" asks Kent.

"The moment you say 'Yes'," Jerry replies.

"Last question," grins Kent. "Money?"

Jerry looks up at Kent, a tear glistening in his eyes. "Man, it was a big decision: it was not bloody easy believe me: I sold my studio and my pad in Aussie."

"Are you serious? And you only *sort of* asked Estella?" says Kent.

Jerry shrugs, "I had plans on joining you anyway."

Kent laughs out loud. "Who says we or Estella want you, you cocky little bastard?"

"I love you, too, mate: go and get stuffed!" says Jerry as Kent holds out his hand: "Welcome to *'TaKeOne Productions*, partner," he says.

Later that afternoon, with the sun nearing the horizon, Tanya and Kent see Jerry Jacobs leave the guesthouse on the wine farm, where he still has a room, jump on a bicycle, and take off in the direction of the nearby village where most of the artisans live.

"Where's he off to?" asks Tanya, leaning over the balustrade of their loft balcony.

"One of two things," speculates Kent, "to hire his construction crew, or to firm up his *sort of* arrangements with Estella and her family," and then he tells Tanya all about the early afternoons meeting.

"I don't believe it!" Tanya smiles. "I knew they had something going; but for him to sell up in Australia and come over here."

"Look who's talking," says Kent.

"But I didn't sell up in Australia!" Tanya protests "I was already travelling when I decided to stop off in South Africa for a while."

"And then, what happened?" he carries on with a grin.

"Then I sold out to a Rooster," she says, joining in his amusement. Then changing the subject, she says: "Now that there are four of us ..."

"Four of us?" says Kent not quite sure what Tanya is getting at.

"Yes, four of us: Jerry, Estella, you and I," she insists and explains further. "They will get married, and you and I, well you know, we are like a couple *sort of* – we all get on, and I really like Estella. Not only is she a good person with an incredible voice, she has music in her veins, like Jerry – like you and me. She is too good to be working in the vineyard, she should be working with us. Help me develop local talent, help organise concerts; there is so much to do!" They sit and talk late into the night.

"She said 'yes' and the carpenters are starting on Monday," says Jerry all in one breath, as he walks into the big studio's control room.

"Who agreed first? Estella or the carpenter?" asks Tanya with a straight face.

Falling for the gibe, Jerry says: "the carpenters were easy; but Estella, that was another story ..." before he realises that the other two are killing themselves laughing.

Somewhat embarrassed, he adds: "Her father was the problem: he was on about losing his daughter's income, and some other BS about me being a white Australian, and his daughter being, you know, a ... a farm worker. I told him: I will give you her wages every week, but he did not want that either. Anyway, it's done and dusted: we are getting hitched when the yurt is finished, and I have a threshold to carry her over."

"Congratulations Jerry," says Kent, then adds: "Go and tell Estella to give her notice on the farm. We anticipated your move when we saw you riding into the village yesterday evening and would like to discuss our ideas with the two of you."

Just then the studio door is pushed open by a smiling Estella. "Pappa told me this morning that I should resign from my farm job to help you with putting up our tent."

"It's not a bloody tent," Jerry protests, "it's a yurt."

"Whatever, I don't care," she laughs. "Jannie, Junior was very nice about it when I told him. He said that seeing it is off-season,

I could go any time. Then he asked me if I was going to become a singer. I told him, no, I am going to marry you."

"Why did you say that? Don't you want to become a singer anymore?" Jerry insists.

"How can I? Married women can't be singers: they have to be sexy and single."

Tanya, Kent, and Jerry all break out in hoots of laughter over Estella's innocent statement and Jerry's smile becomes broader still when Kent and Tanya repeat the relevant points of their previous night's discussions:

- Jerry will take over the recording studio;
- Since Estella does not only have a beautiful voice, but also a good ear and strong leadership potential, Tanya will teach her how to become a DJ, a re-mixer and a talent coach;
- Kent will supervise the yurt construction, as he feels best qualified to minimise the environmental impact of this type of green building and – depending on the outcome of the first yurt, he has bigger plans for an adjoining property;
- They agree to set the date for the first concert to coincide with the completion of the next grape harvest.

Not a week later Jerry gets the news that Estella's *Acapella* rendition of "Bohemian Rhapsody" has entered the Australian charts at number fifteen. Jerry and Tanya put all else on hold to complete Estella debut album: Estella – Just One Voice to be released by *TaKeOne Productions* in Australia.

Meanwhile Lizzy, Abby, Gwyn, Jacob, Mannie and Luke – Estella's vineyard farming friends have worked on a Commodores Songbook that include hits by Marvin Gaye and Lionel Ritchie, which Kent records in the big sound studio and mixes upstairs in the loft on Tanya's old equipment to keep out of the way.

"You know we are working harder than ever before," says Tanya one night, way after midnight, "but honestly, Rooster, I have never had so much fun and satisfaction. These locals are like sponges, soaking it all in. It's amazing!"

"Weren't we just like that – you and me – when we first started out?" replies Kent, pulling her under the duvet cover of their hand-crafted bed.

"Jerry, the carpenter is here, let us go up to your clearing and set out your floorplan," says Kent, leaning into the control room door.

"Right with you," replies Jerry, gesturing to Tanya that he is leaving the controls to her. Once outside, they walk up the natural slope of the amphitheatre; veer off onto the narrow path that takes them to the sparkling pool, with the rock overhang behind it.

"I can see why you picked this spot," says Bernie, the carpenter, who has a copy of the blueprint on a clipboard under his arm. Considering the decagon, or ten-sided shape of the raised floor platform, he nods his head in approval: "I am glad it's not round like the yurt that will sit on it."

Measuring the clearing under the overhang, he says: "Twelve metres will fit nicely, leaving you a two-point-five metre boardwalk all the way around a seven-metre yurt. Plus: it allows for an expansion to a twelve-metre diameter yurt once the kids start popping up," he smirks at Jerry.

"We will drive one-point-two metre by fifty-mil rebars one metre into the ground, where they will anchor the 500-mil logs we pre-drill to press onto the rebar. That's our foundation: no concrete or brickwork and easy to move anytime Jerry feels like a change of scenery or wants a conventional house instead of a nomad's yurt."

"Wait until it is finished before casting a verdict," says Jerry, slapping the old carpenter affectionately on the back.

Next, they go over the trellis for the walls; the skeleton of the dome, and the two windows on either side of the door.

"That's all the carpentry in place. We have made up and treated all the pieces in my workshop already; we will start tomorrow and should be done in three days."

"Then I better get going with the trenches for the services right away and re-instate the plants the moment the pipes and cables have been laid and tested," says Kent.

"What about the cover?" asks Bernie.

"I have got heavy-duty, grey PVC tarpaulins from the trucking company and a PVC welder. Once the skeleton is up, we can cut the segments and weld them together. Then all we need is some muscle to pull the bathing cap over the skull; fit the polycarbonate ventilation cone, and we are watertight," says Kent and then, turning to Jerry, he adds: "Move in your furniture and carry your bride over the threshold before the end of the month."

From then on, the pace increases all round. The sale of the wine estate is finalised and the date for the Harvest Festival is set.
Apart from their own signed artists, Tanya signs contracts with the Cape Town Symphony Orchestra and rehearsals get under way.
Having been thrown into the deep end, Estella copes surprisingly well in assisting Tanya, while simultaneously organising her wedding day with her mother and selecting the furniture with Jerry for their yurt which is nearing completion.

Chapter Thirty-One

Carla

With three chairs and a rickety table set up outside Carla's Passage Hairdressing Salon, Christian is quickly joined by a steady stream of regular shoppers that come for fresh bread on their right and Danish cheeses on their left. Much to the amusement of younger shoppers, the group even add their own fold-up chairs to Christian's to form an ever fluctuating circle.

Christian regales them with yarns of his 40 years spent in "Darkest Africa, where lion and rhinoceros walked through my backyard".

"Pappa," his daughter admonishes him, "there were no lions or rhinos in your backyard in the East Rand."

"Do you think these old folks know that, or care?" her father grins. "They come and listen to me prattle on, so that they have a bed-time story to tell their grandkids, instead of reading from the old fairy tales of the Brothers Grimm."

Carla smiles to herself and carries on packing new stocks of hair products on display shelves that Pablo has put up for her under the stairs.

After agreeing to rent the narrow "passage shop" and the two-bedroom apartment behind it, and paying six months' rent in advance, their move had taken less than a week. In the meantime, Theresa has sublet her parents' apartment virtually overnight. The removers had packed the furniture and belongings that Christian and Carla had wanted to have in Faxe Ladeplads in one day. When father and daughter had arrived on the bus at the port entrance on the following morning, the removers already had been waiting for them.

The best news, however, had come from Pablo, who had stuck his head into her kitchen as she was unpacking a box of cooking utensils, plates, cups, and saucers.

"You won't be needing those often," he said, "unless you are a dedicated chef."

"Decidedly not," she had replied, before he had continued.

"The Marina Restaurant, which is run by Joren and Inge," he explained, "serves an excellent smorgasbord at lunchtime and varying dinner specials every night. It's cheaper than to cook yourself."

Carla had liked the sound of that and the two of them strolled the short distance across to the Marina restaurant daily. Joren (the chef) and Inge, who served them at the table, were a lovely couple, making them more than welcome, once they had made the connection to the hair salon. In fact, after less than a week, Christian and Carla invariably shared a table with locals or visiting yachties.

Theresa had also been a great help: she had secured two swivel/reclining hairdressing chairs, two basins, two large wall mirrors, and a hairdresser's trolley at auction.

One of Pablo's friends, who was a handyman, or Mr Fixit, had put up a throughflow geyser and had fitted the basins and extra electric sockets after hours. Re-directing Pablo's spotlights, he had installed to illuminate the artist's landscapes, he had turned the salon into a bright, cheerful place.

In the end, Carla's core business had not come from among the permanent residents, but from the visiting yachts that often moored in the marina to stock up with provisions or carry out repairs to their boats.

Surprisingly, Pablo's initial curiosity in Carla had faded when she had kept his advances at arms' length, using the need to care for her father as an excuse.

I really don't need to add a struggling painter to my list of conquests, she had mused.

During these more recent days, everything was going well for them. Theresa had visited them during the day from time to time to satisfy herself that her father and younger sister were managing on their own and she had enjoyed the Marina restaurant's food with them. Carla had transferred the money from the sale of her house in the Cape to her Danish bank, and – together with Kent's monthly alimony payments – had added the amount to her hairdressing income, and they had been living quite well.

"Fader?" Carla calls out one morning, knocking on his closed bedroom door. With her first client of the day washed, cut and blow-dried, she is surprised not to have heard him outside in his usual seat.

"Pappa?" *Has he gone to the bakery for croissants, his favourite?* Not spotting him in the bakery, or the dairy on the other side of her salon, she tries his bedroom door again. Opening it slowly, she is met by quiet and darkness, with the shutters still firmly closed. Finding the light switch on the wall next to the door, she switches it on.

"PAPPA! PAPPA!"

"Theresa, it's Carla," she sobs, as if her sister does not recognise her voice. "Pappa passed away in his sleep last night. Are you there? Pappa is dead."

"Heart attack," confirms the doctor, that Pablo had summonsed in response to Carla's cries for help. "He died in his sleep."

Inge consoles the sisters when she takes some food across to them.

In this small community, the hurried visit by a doctor, followed by an ambulance, does not go unnoticed and is the main topic of the day. "Christian Carstens from Africa has passed away," the news spreads like wildfire.

"How old was he?"

"Eighty-eight, eighty-nine? He had a good run – went peacefully in his sleep."

Soon after the funeral, Inge and Joren convince Carla that life must go on, and that she should re-open her salon.

A framed picture of her, flanked by Anna and Christian Carstens on the veranda of the Cape house, taken by Leonora the day her parents had left South Africa, takes pride of place on the sideboard between the two salon mirrors.

What am I still doing here? she asks herself. *I came here for him. Where can I go? Copenhagen? Join my spinster sister?* These thoughts continue to torment her day and night.

"Do you cut men's hair?" asks a tousle-haired, deeply tanned man, maybe in his sixties.

"Yes, I do," responds Carla, getting out of one of the two hairdresser's chairs she normally used to rest her legs between clients. Rolling down the polo neck of his thick-knitted pullover, she secures the paper cravat, before slipping the apron over him.

"How would you like it cut?" she asks, looking at him in the mirror.

His deep blue eyes crinkle in a smile: "About half off, I guess. Have not had the luxury of a proper hairdresser for a while."

Combing through his wavy hair, she says: "Not too bad. You want me to wash it? Apply some conditioner? The sun has had a field day on your head: you should wear a hat or a cap of sorts."

He laughs: "Lady, do you know how many caps I have donated to the Seven Seas?"

Against her will, she finds herself laughing, visualising him at the helm of his boat, grabbing in vain after yet another cap.

"Lady, you laugh: do you know how much a half-decent cap costs these days?"

"Please stop calling me 'lady': my name is Carla Fowler ... I mean Carla Carstens."

He sits up so unexpectedly, she nearly cuts a thick tuft of his hair away.

"Carla who?" he asks, studying her intently.

"Carla Carstens," she repeats.

"Sorry Carla, before you corrected yourself, I heard you say 'Fowler'. Is that right?" he insists.

Now already irritated by this stranger, she replies curtly: "Yes, you heard right, Fowler was my married name. I have since divorced and reverted to my maiden name. Have you got a problem with that?"

Sensing her rising anger, the stranger says: "I'm sorry to have offended you. Please, finish cutting my hair and then allow me to explain myself over lunch, yes?"

Looking at her wristwatch she says, more out of curiosity: "12.30: lunch sounds good."

When she brushes at his pullover, having relieved him of the protective apron, she says: "The Marina restaurant serves a good smorgasbord."

"Yes, it is very good, but my crew caught some soles last night that need eating. Let us have lunch on my yacht."

Closing the door of the salon, she flips the 'CLOSED' sign over, on the back of which she had written 'BACK IN 29 MINUTES'. He looks at the sign and smiles, before saying: "I think you are cutting it rather fine."

Chapter Thirty-Two

Kent & Tanya

The Dutch Reformed Church is bursting: every seat is taken, with more people craning their necks at the open doors. Loudspeakers have been hastily set up outside, as an afterthought, to relay the sermon. Supplementing the small organ are the six Acapella farm singers, who have recorded their first album, calling themselves "The Bokmakieries", much to the local community's amusement, being very familiar with the little bird's distinctive call.

Estella, dressed in a long white dress, is standing nervously next to her father, who dressed in his Sunday church-going suit. In the pews behind them are her mother, her brothers and sisters, and the rest of the Kleynhans family. On the other side of the centre aisle stands Tanya with Jannie Myburgh, Junior, his wife Annelise and the rest of the Myburgh clan.

Kent is standing among the people, craning to get a look inside, but he is not looking inside the church. He is looking up the Main Road, waiting as the appointed best man for the groom. At first, he had stood in his allocated seat in the front pew, but after driving around the block for close on fifteen minutes, Mr Kleynhans had resolutely taken his daughter Estella inside, and told Kent to wait for the wayward groom outside.

Perched on the back of a bakkie, with his bicycle next to him, Jerry stops at the kerb, handing his bike to a young bystander.

"Bloody flat tyre, mate," he says to Kent, dusting down his off-white suit. "You got the rings?" he asks, as they push their way through the crowd standing in the open door.

"Yes," says Kent, as The Bokmakieries take their cue and start up with "Here Comes the Bride" which brings on a round of raucous laughter from the congregation.

"Good start," groans Jerry, with Kent now leading him to stand next to Estella.

All proceeds well until the priest asks the couple the customary question: "Will you, Jerome Nicolas Jacobs take ..." when Estella interrupts in her clear, strong voice: "Who? Jerome Nicolas? Is that your name Jerry?" The microphone carries her words clearly over the sound system for everyone to hear. Another round of laughter stops the ceremony for more than a minute.

Later on, the community hall is far too small. The number of self-invited guests outnumbers the fifty invited guests by more than four to one.

Nobody cares – *'n party is mos 'n party, nê?* – blankets are spread on the rugby field next to the community hall993, more sound speakers are set up outside and the dancing begins outside long before the bridal couple have had their opening dance.

Nobody knows where all the food and drink is coming from; especially the wine, and it is definitely not non-alcoholic outside, that's for sure.

By eight o'clock, the Myburgh family bid the bridal couple "good luck and good night" to return to their respective estates. Estella leans across to Kent, who has his car parked higher up in front of the police station, "Can we go now? I want to see my tent." Breaking into more laughter she adds: "and Jerome Nicolas must carry me over the crashhold."

Jerry winces good-naturedly: "It's a yurt, my darling, with a threshold."

"Whatever, just do it, Jerome Nicolas Jacobs!"

"I must say, this was the best and funniest wedding I have ever been to," Tanya gasps as Kent and her climb up the spiral staircase to their loft. Opening the sliding doors and stepping out onto their balcony, they can just make out the two white-clad figures lit by the light of their torch as they veer off onto the narrow path leading to their yurt.

Only when Kent closes the triple-glazed sliding doors of their loft does the music from the grounds of the community hall become blocked out completely.

"Have you also got more first names Kent Fowler that I should know about before ...?" Tanya asks without entirely completing the sentence.

"Before what?" asks Kent, raising himself on one elbow on the bed.

"Before I register you as the illegitimate father of our child," says Tanya, smiling up at him from her pillow.

"You are not ...?"

"Oh, yes I am, Mister Rooster, and you have six months to decide if the surname is going to be 'Fowler' or Dudnic."

"Dudnic? Is that your name? I thought it was 'Hot Stuff'", he says pulling her gently into his arms.

Chapter Thirty-Three

TaKeOne Night

The first overseas visitors to arrive at the Klein Drakenstein Valley Estate are Dorothy and Graham Fowler. Meeting his parents in the entrance of the Wine Estate, all Kent needs to do is stand back: the black, reflective-glass building, with its sloping masonry walls, natural amphitheatre, and majestic Klein Drakenstein backdrop does all the talking. Finally standing on the balcony of the loft, his parents are overwhelmed by what has been achieved in such a short time, and how tastefully it has all been executed. Throwing her arms around Tanya, Dorothy exclaims: "This is beautiful! Graham, I want to live here."

Feigning exasperation, Graham says to Kent, loud enough for the two women to hear: "Last month, after I finished the restoration of Madge's house, she told me: 'This is it, Graham, I am never going to move again.'"

"Maybe six months here; six months there – follow the swallows," says Kent, smiling meaningfully at Tanya.

Jerry and Estella, who had joined the Fowlers, Kent, and Tanya in the recording studio, wasted no time in taking the Fowlers to their yurt.

"Well, I never!" Graham exclaims, "It's barely visible under this overhang of rock."

"Look at the space and the comfort inside: it's better than a five-star hotel," Dorothy adds. "I could live here."

"Give us half an hour to unpack, then we expect a tour of your property on the other side of the road," says Graham. "I'll phone you: my old sim card still has time on it, and I am sure you have things to do."

That, of course, had been a typically British understatement. Ever since the wedding, the last few weeks have pushed everyone to their limit. Fortunately, the Cape Town Symphony Orchestra's conductor, Dylan de Witt, a relatively young, but highly progressive conductor to be appointed to the post had decided to have the rehearsals in Cape Town, with a dress rehearsal two nights before the concert.

Tanya, Kent, Jerry, and Estella, who by this time had become very much an integral part of *TaKeOne Productions*, had chosen to devote their premier concert entirely to local talent. Leaving the choice of songs to suit their personal talent, Dylan de Witt had engaged a few top voice coaches and choreographers to ensure that these fledgling artists were ready for the occasion.

The premier's billboard: *'One Night to Remember'* had been punted on the social media as "The Klein Drakenstein's Charity Event of the Year". With only 1,000 tickets available at a price of R1,000 (just under US $75) per ticket, they were sold out in hours.

During their first intimate dinner in the wine estate's private dining room, presided over by Ahmed, Tanya nudges Kent. "Will you – or must I?" she urges.

"What is it dear?" asks Dorothy. Taking Dorothy's and Graham's hands, she says: "It's not a leap year, but I'll ask anyway: Do you mind if I *sort of* marry your son?"

Picking up on her choice of words, Graham asks: "*Sort of?*"

"Yes, *sort of*, because he has not asked me yet – but with his baby on the way, I need to make sure it's a Fowler, don't you agree?"

With Estella and Jerry joining the four of them the following evening for dinner, the conversation turns to their collective plans for the future.

"Estella has risen to Number Three on the Australian charts with her single, "I Heard It Through the Grapevine", and her album, *Estella – One Voice*, has just entered the album charts," says Jerry proudly.

Blushing a deep red, Estella murmurs: "Do you have to brag, Jerome Nicolas?"

Laughing, Tanya relates the wedding incident to the amused Fowlers.

"Are you going to sing in the concert?" asks Dorothy.

"Yes, I will," says the girl," but only a few songs, because there are so many talented people in our community, we could sing all night."

Right on cue, Jerry gets up to open the sliding doors to the veranda, where the six Bokmakieries are standing to sing their *Acapella* version of the Commodores' hit song, "Nightshift." Dorothy spontaneously breaks into tears. "Better bring a man-size hankie to the concert if you cry like that after just one song," says Estella passing her a cotton napkin.

Next to arrive are Jerry's friends and family from Australia. With the guesthouse filled to capacity, some have to be quartered in nearby B&Bs.

"When are you coming to Aussie?" asks his brother Teddy, who has taken over Jerry's studio at a special discounted price.

Looking around to check if Estella is within earshot, he whispers: "Not a word to Estella before the concert; she'll be too excited to sing. *TaKeOne Productions*, our recording company, has signed for an Australian tour of six cities and twelve concerts. You can look out for us."

DJ Mumbo Jumbo and his girl Cherry fly in from LA, listen to most of the music recorded in the studio so far and promise to alert all-night stations in the USA.

"Hey, Rooster, when this concert is over, we must hire some help," says Tanya, rubbing her tummy.

"Yes," says Kent, "hang in there: dress rehearsals tomorrow, then last-day adjustments, and then we are on."

The thousand guests fill the amphitheatre very nicely.

With an excited buzz in the air, most folks are spread out on their blankets or pieces of canvas. In front of the stage, two rows of folding chairs have been set up, to which Graham and Dorothy have been escorted and are joined by the Myburgh clan, with Jannie, Junior, making the introductions.

The Cape Town Symphony Orchestra is positioned at the rear of the tiered stage, leaving ample space for the performing groups and solo artists up front. As the last of the evening sun's rays illuminate the mountain tops, the floodlights flare up and bathe the stage in soft swirls of autumn colours. A pencil spot accompanies Dylan de Witt to his position at the foot of his orchestra. After a deep bow to the audience, he turns to the expectant musicians and taps his baton on the podium. Immediately, those tuning their instruments grind to a halt, and he raises his baton.

A medley of tunes, based on the later performances by the individual artists fills the amphitheatre, to be greeted by a polite smattering of applause for the more popular tunes. The stage lighting fades as the last bars of the medley reverberate through the gorge, followed by a hushed silence. Unnoticed by most, a black, full-width screen descends from the ceiling, hiding de Witt and his orchestra entirely. A single spotlight illuminates the tall, slender figure of Estella.

Sheathed in a silvery-white, full-length gown, she stands alone in the darkness, centre stage. Her long, black hair is heavily braided with silvery extensions that frame her head in a sparkling glow. Softly, the symphony orchestra begins with the opening chords, to stop dead the moment Estella's clear voice breaks forth.

Nights in white satin ...

As she proceeds – instead of the full orchestra joining in, her own projected image lights up on the screen next to Estella, to be joined by another projection. Singing in harmony, on the other side of the lone figure on stage.

Confusion spreads through the audience when yet a further two life-size "Estellas" appear on the screen. The illusory "Quintet of Estella's" singing in *Acapella* harmony was Jerry's idea when he was overlaying the tracks he had, one by one, recorded with Estella in the iso-booth.

"Why don't I project you onto the screen like a hologram of yourself?" he had suggested.

The effect on stage is breathtakingly beautiful. When the orchestra rejoins Estella during the closing bars of the song, the audience is already on its feet with the first standing ovation of the night.

During the next one and a half hours, local groups and solo artists perform with the backing of the orchestra. As the gala evening comes to an end, The Bokmakieries take centre stage in front of the screen to render their cover of Marvin Gaye.

Jerry superimposes the sextet to fill the width of the stage, as – one by one – the night's performers join them on stage, welcomed by further applause and loud cheers.

Last, but not least, the *TaKeOne Production* team – Tanya,

Kent, Estella, and Jerry – enter the stage through the door to the recording studios.

As they take their bows to thunderous applause, Dillon de Witt raises his baton for the orchestra's *Grand Finalé*.

Chapter Thirty-Four

Carla

"That's some yacht you got there, Mister."

"I do apologize for my lack of manners, it's Ellerine – Ottmar Ellerine," he says, giving her a hand up the gangplank to the deck of his gleaming wooden yacht "Ysterfontein".

Turning to a young man who is busy polishing the yacht's large brass bell, he says: "Frikkie, please tell Ilse that we have a guest for lunch." Then he turns back to Carla and says: "Before we sit down, let me show you my yacht."

It takes Ottmar fifteen minutes to show Carla around and to introduce her to the four crew members: Frikkie, the first mate; Ilse, the chef; Catharine; and Benny. Sitting at the lunch table, which has been set under an awning on the aft-deck, Ottmar pours her a glass of iced lemon tea and says: "Before I tell you more about us, I am curious to hear more from you Missus Fowler."

"Why does the name 'Fowler' intrigue you?" Carla asks, getting annoyed once more at his persistence.

"Because I believe we may have a common past acquaintance."

When Carla raises her eyebrows in a quizzical look Ottmar tells her about the DJ couple to whom he had sold his wine estate in the Klein Drakenstein Valley. "It is a small world, Carla," he concludes, trying to judge her reaction.

Carla sits in utter silence throughout their excellent meal of pan-fried lemon sole, boiled baby potatoes, and a crisp green salad. She declines his offer of a glass of Cape Riesling, until he assures her that it is non-alcoholic.

"Alcohol and yachts don't sail well together," he smiles.

Returning his smile, she utters: "Forty years of memories came flooding back."

"We all have them," he says. "That is no reason to stop gathering new ones. Life is too short for regrets. Look at your achievements and count your blessings."

The soft chirp alerts her to the time, and her next client. Walking her to the Marina entrance, Ottmar says: "I am treating my crew for dinner at the Marina Restaurant tonight. Why don't you join us?"

I could do with some company, she thinks, and accepts his offer to meet them at 7.30 pm.

As it happens, Joren sticks his head into the salon after purchasing more cheeses next door.

"See you later, Joren," she tells him. "I have been invited out for dinner by Ottmar and his crew, you know, that big yacht, the 'Ysterfontein'?"

Joren whistles through his teeth. "Do you know him?" he says in disbelief. "He insists on bringing his own non-alcoholic wine. Crew don't drink either. Pulls in here because our marina is deep enough for his boat. Has been in and out all summer; most likely to leave soon for warmer climates." With a wave and a "see you later", he gets on his way.

Soon to leave for warmer climates? Carla muses. *I wish I could do that.*

A couple of minutes after the arranged time, she joins Ottmar and his crew at their table after waving to Inge and Joren at the kitchen counter.

Rising to his feet immediately Ottmar smiles at her: "In case you have forgotten, may I introduce you to Frikkie, Ilse, Catharine, and Benny. All of them signed on in Cape Town after I rebuilt the yacht."

Being completely at home among the all-South African crew, Carla feels herself starting to relax for the first time since her father had passed away. The conversation makes the rounds with everyone taking turns to relate some highlights from their previous journeys. Ottmar, the ever-observant host, proceeds to outline their immediate plans.

"Two or three more days here," he explains, "then down to the Mediterranean, through the Suez, and then we toss a coin. Heads we go up to Asia; tails we go down the coast of Africa, including Mauritius, Seychelles, Madagascar ..."

"Stop, please stop, Ottmar," Carla begs, "you are making me dizzy with envy. I wish I were on your crew."

"Be very careful what you wish for," Frikkie admonishes her, to everyone's amusement.

"We could do with a world-champion hairdresser on board," Ilse grumbles, pulling on her swept-up hair.

Joining in the light-hearted banter, Carla says: "Where would I sleep?"

"We'll put up a hammock on the aft-deck for you," suggests Frikkie.

Looking with a cheeky grin at Ottmar, Catherine says: "The captain could move over in his king-size bed."

The ensuing silence is shattered by Ottmar's straight-faced reply: "I could live with that. Want to give it a try, Carla?"

Blushing a deep scarlet, Carla looks from one crew member to the other until her eyes rest on Ottmar: "I think I can live with that, too!"

Three days later, Catherine, Inge, and Benny each hold one of Carla's cases, while she shuts the glass salon door and turns the sign on the front door over once again from 'BACK IN 29 MINUTES' to 'CLOSED'.

THE END

9 781776 428878